N[illegible]

He had made one [illegible] rayne had believed his pursuers when they shouted up at him that if he came out from among the rocks and surrendered, they would take him back to be tried by a judge and a jury.

He showed his face, and a bullet splintered a rock a few inches from his head.

That told him all he had to know.

The men after him didn't want to take him alive. They were murderers. They wanted to kill him. Kill him if they could.

Not that easy they wouldn't.

Bryan Drayne was done with dodging bullets. It was time to turn the killing game around. . .

The Ballad of Bryan Drayne

Frank Roderus

A SIGNET BOOK
NEW AMERICAN LIBRARY

PUBLISHER'S NOTE

This book is a work of fiction. Names, characters, places, and incidents are either the product of the author's imagination or are used fictitiously, and any resemblance to actual persons, living or dead, events, or locales is entirely coincidental.

SIGNET TRADEMARK REG. U.S.PAT. OFF. AND FOREIGN COUNTRIES
REGISTERED TRADEMARK—MARCA REGISTRADA
HECHO EN CHICAGO, U.S.A.

SIGNET, SIGNET CLASSIC, MENTOR, ONYX, PLUME, MERIDIAN and NAL BOOKS are published by NAL PENGUIN INC., 1633 Broadway, New York, New York 10019

First Printing, November, 1987

1 2 3 4 5 6 7 8 9

PRINTED IN THE UNITED STATES OF AMERICA

for Jim Dewey

Chapter 1

His fingers, his hands, were shaking, but he could not feel them. He could only see that they were. There was almost no feeling left past the heel of his palms. Trying to manipulate the sulfur-tipped match between those raw, pale, oddly remote little stubs was like trying to hold the thing between a pair of sticks. He had to move his fingers by sight and not feel, like some infernal machine. But he had to make it work. He had to get the match lit. He *had* to.

Frustrated, he rocked back on his heels and closed his eyes for a moment in quiet supplication. It was not a prayer, really. He was begging.

He opened his eyes and leaned forward, trying to cup the upper part of his body around the nest of twigs and dried grasses he had dug out of a tiny crack in the mottled gray-and-red rocks. The nest had been abandoned long ago by whatever animal or bird had built it. Drayne did not know enough about such things to know or to care what had constructed the nest. What he did know was that this ragged assortment of burnable material was now his only chance for survival.

Still working by feel, he struck the match against a stone. Friction created the heat he needed, and the tip burst into flame.

He resisted an impulse to warm his hands around the match flare and instead shoved the flame into the dried and crumbly remains of the old nest.

Sprigs of grass caught first, curling and quickly turning black, falling into useless ash before the brief spark of fire could spread to a more substantial fuel. Drayne wanted to weep.

He pushed the match stem forward, shoving it deeper into the nest. Flame licked at the tip of his index finger, but he could barely feel it. The small amount of sensation that he could feel was actually welcome.

A twig caught and then another.

With a glad racking sob of relief he snatched his hand away from the fire and tipped the ball-like nest on edge so the fire could spread through the combustible material.

Working quickly now, he scrabbled on the stone of the ledge for more of the weathered sticks and limbs he had gathered, grabbing them up and laying them over the small fire until he threatened to smother it.

The wood caught. One stick and then another. One piece feeding another and larger bit until the whole pile was burning with a swift, blessedly hot rush.

Drayne squeezed his eyes shut and leaned wearily against the wall of stone at his side.

Heat from the still-growing fire reflected off the rock and surrounded him. Weak with relief as much as from the exhaustion that had nearly overcome him, he held his hands out, soaking up heat.

Drayne opened his shirt, unbuttoned it to the waist, and held the cloth wide, not wanting anything to remain between his skin and the heat, wanting to be able to soak up every available bit of warmth.

His fingers hurt, particularly from the tips to the first joints, as the heat soaked in beneath the surface of his skin. He wondered just how close he had come to frostbite.

He had not thought to worry about anything like that until now. When he set out early in the fall, it had not seemed especially cold.

But then, when he set out he had not been thinking in terms of weather either.

Besides, it was not the air temperature that had gotten to him. It was that fall in the creek. The chill of the water had not seemed so bad at the time, but the effects had been lingering. The seat of his trousers and his crotch were still damp.

He turned his back to the fire and wondered if he had

time enough to take his pants off and dry them over the flame.

Someone, one of *them*, was likely to see the smoke from down below.

He added wood to the fire and looked up, up past the cliff that he still needed to climb. There was little smoke from the dry wood. But there was some. He could barely see it against the sky, but the thin, pale wisps were much more visible against dark, dull stone. He reminded himself that the men down below would be looking at the smoke against a backdrop of sheer rock. He had to assume that they could see, that they must know where he was.

The biggest question was whether any of them would attempt the difficult climb he had just made. Or if they would stay with the dogs and the horses, try to circle around somehow to get above and behind him.

The logical thing for them to do, he thought, would be to split the party. Send two or three up the rocks, and maybe leave another few down below to keep watch while the rest of them tried to circle around.

They would have the advantage of knowing the country, too. Drayne had no idea if there was an easy access to the mountaintop from the canyon floor. His pursuers would know.

He shivered, not from cold this time but from the fear that was returning.

He had been so miserable for the past half hour or so that he had almost forgotten how frightened he was. He added more wood to his fire, even though it was already larger than he really needed, hoping the heat would drive away fear as well as cold.

He leaned away from the rock, wishing he had some thing to hold on to, and looked down over the side. The sight of the sharp drop made his stomach churn in protest. He was amazed at his precipitous route up the sheer face of rock and quickly looked away. His hands were warmer now, and the prickling, tingling sensation subsided and was replaced by acute pains as he became aware of the raw red sores and abrasions that covered fingers, palms, and wrists.

Soon his hands would begin to stiffen. And he knew the pain would be worse come morning when he had to use his hands and break the scabs that would be forming.

If he was still alive in the morning.

For a moment he felt hopeless, a helpless resignation come over him. It would be so easy to give up now and let them take him.

He forced himself to snap out of it. He would *not* let them come fetch him like some rabbit frozen in terror. He would not.

He swore it. But even as he did so he could feel himself begin to sob, could feel the convulsive shaking of his shoulders.

It was not really even the hopelessness of his situation that he minded. As long as he was alive and free, he reminded himself, there had to be some measure of hope remaining.

What he minded the most about his situation was the complete and utter unfairness of it.

There was no *reason* for it.

But no one seemed to care. No one seemed to *want* to know. Fury had replaced reason, and he had no hope at all that anyone would stop to listen to him. Not one of them.

They were on a blood hunt now, every one of the fools, chasing him with all the intensity and fierce pleasure of small boys chasing after a barn rat. Except that these overgrown children were using revolvers and repeating rifles instead of sharpened sticks.

And Bryan Drayne was the rat they had cornered.

He shivered again and added wood to the fire.

Chapter 2

It started over a piece of pie. A piece of *pie,* for God's sake.

The man in the way station asked if he wanted a piece of hot pie to go with his coffee, and Drayne said that he would. It sounded good. He was not particularly hungry, but he was tired. A piece of hot apple pie sounded like a fine pick-me-up on a chilly, overcast afternoon.

Hot from the oven? he had asked.

Fresh, the man assured him.

He nodded and the man turned away, back into the kitchen.

The man had been back there much longer than it would have taken just to cut a piece of pie and put it onto a plate, but Drayne had been in no hurry.

And while the man was in back, there were sounds of an argument, voices rising sharp and loud, a man's and a woman's.

So the fellow had a scrap with his wife or employee or whatever. The fact had not seemed significant at the time although Drayne realized now that the argument had soured the man's mood by the time he finally returned with the pie he had talked Drayne into.

It was then that Drayne made his mistake, although he couldn't have guessed its consequences.

The pie, instead of being hot from the oven, was in that lukewarm state between cold and hot when the flavors are at their worst. Hot would have been delicious; cold would have been acceptable, but the in-between temperature was just plain bad.

Drayne tasted the stuff and pushed it away with a

mumbled complaint. Not loud. Just a murmur of displeasure.

He wished now that he had shouted and ranted about it. At least that would have drawn the attention of the others in the room.

At least then someone would have been paying attention and might have understood what happened.

But as it was the only person who seemed to hear was the way-station proprietor.

That man's anger was dangling by such a fine thread that it took nothing more than Drayne's softly spoken criticism of the pie to set him off.

The man whirled, face flushed with anger that spread across his neck and cheeks and pulled the corners of his eyes tight.

Whatever argument he had just had in private was now carried into the public room and exploded onto the customer seated at his counter.

Like some wild animal, he lurched forward, clawing for Drayne's throat.

Drayne was more startled than frightened. He had no time for fear. Not then.

He reacted instinctively, throwing his arms up to ward off the man's attack.

There had been a struggle. Drayne could not even now begin to piece it together in his memory. It was too fast, too unexpected. The man lunged for him and Drayne responded, battering and smashing and cursing across the planed but unvarnished wood of the counter. Funny how Drayne more clearly remembered the shape and color and texture of the pie saucer and fork than he did the face of the man he had fought. He remembered the smell of the man's breath and the tickle of his hair against his cheek but not what the man looked like.

The whole thing was so brief. In seconds the man was down on the floor with bright, shiny blood flowing from a split in his scalp.

Drayne reasoned—now—that the man fell and struck his head on the sharp corner of a zinc washtub behind the counter.

Even that, though, he was not certain about. It was

an assumption based on what little he remembered from the scuffle and what he saw behind the counter afterward.

He remembered a tuft of mustache hair that needed trimming on the right side of the man's mouth. But he recalled no details of the scuffle at all. A push to fend off the man's hands. A fall. It was the only reasonable explanation.

But no one else in the room was interested in reason.

There had been a chilling hush in the place after the man went down. An unnatural silence. And someone went behind the counter to check on the man who lay there.

"My God," the man whispered into the silence of the room. "Harry's dead. This man has killed Harry."

Immediately there was a palpable change in the atmosphere of the place, though nothing was said. Drayne could still remember with total clarity the sudden *feel* inside that large room. The place seethed with an intense animal rage that brought a prickling to the back of his neck.

Someone behind him shouted, "Get him," and a dozen pairs of hands reached for him.

Perhaps he should have tried to explain.

He did not.

He bolted instead, ducking away from the men who were reaching for him and rushing for the door. For escape.

A howl went up from the men in the room like the baying of hounds on a fresh scent.

Drayne remembered someone grabbing at his sleeve.

He remembered throwing an elbow into another man's face and the quick spurt of blood that followed.

Hands grabbed, clutched, and were torn away as he charged, spinning and smashing, toward the door.

That door had seemed the only measure of safety anywhere in the world, and he ran for it with desperate concentration.

He reached it and slipped through as men shouted and threatened and cursed.

He ran blindly, as hard as he could, away from the

coach and the men who were changing the team in the traces, away from everything he owned, away from the coat he had removed and laid on the stool beside him. Away.

Panicked, he admitted to himself now.

But the man had been dead, and no one else in that room had been interested in explanations about how or why it happened.

Their response was as instinctive and unreasoning as his own defense against the man called Harry.

In the space of a heartbeat Drayne had become a fugitive.

And he was frightened now. Lord God, he was frightened.

He closed his eyes tight, trying to shut away thought and memory, trying to wipe out all that had happened in the past few hours. He leaned back against the now-warm wall of the rock at his back.

He was so tired. And so scared. And he did not know how to make any of it right again.

He used the back of his hand to wipe moisture away from his eyes and pulled his shirt closed against a chill that the fire's heat didn't seem to reach.

Chapter 3

Tom Whelan leaned forward, helped himself to a refill from the bottle of rye Lou Kirkland had left on the table, and then leaned back again to tilt his chair against the wall and watch the proceedings before him.

Anyone coming on the scene fresh would have guessed that the men were preparing for a bear hunt. Rifles and whiskey bottles were being lugged around in roughly equal numbers. And the voices that were rising from and between the different groups of people were loud, excited, and eager.

Business was booming tonight. Whelan held back the thin smile that tugged at his lips when the thought came to him that Harry would have loved it.

Across the room the new widow, dry-eyed and busy, was breaking open a fresh case of bottles and handing them out almost faster than she could accept payment for them. Well, not *that* fast, Whelan conceded. She wasn't likely to lose track of anything where profits were involved.

He tilted his hat back off his forehead and took a sip of the rye. It wasn't bad, so he had another.

Kirkland came back and splashed some of the whiskey into his cup. He looked like he was wound tight enough to bust.

"Best get yourself ready, Tom. We pull out at dawn."

Whelan shrugged. He was not interested in committing himself to the company of a bunch of drunks. So far he had seen more whiskey bottles than cartridges loaded into the packs and panniers and saddlebags that the men kept dragging through the place, and food was definitely of minor interest. The place was like a damned carnival.

"You are coming with us, ain't you, Tom?" Kirkland demanded.

"Haven't decided yet, Lou."

"Hell, man, you got to come. Everybody's going. Bill Feeney brought his dogs over this afternoon, and the Archer boy was sent off to get the sheriff. But we figure to have the sonofabitch before the sheriff ever gets here. If he bothers to come at all, that is. Not that we need him. We'll have the bastard by tomorra noon. And you got to be in on it, Tom. It's the most excitement we've had around here since Cousin Kate put her cat through the wringer." Kirkland was half shot already and was grinning. "Besides, Tom, you're the best shot of anybody I know. You got to be with us."

"We'll see," Whelan said. He slouched a little lower in his chair and took another sip of Kirkland's whiskey.

"You got to, Tom."

"Do you figure to hang him or shoot him when you catch him, Lou?"

"Shit, we don't know. We can decide that later, I expect. It depends, I reckon."

"I don't know," Whelan said with a straight face. "Could be dangerous work. The man could be armed. He might turn on you like a catamount once you get him cornered."

"I know," Kirkland said seriously. "That's why we need you, Tom. You being such a hand with a gun. I heard he's packing a couple pistols anyhow, and somebody else said he grabbed up a rifle as he run off. That's why you just got to be with us. You know?"

Whelan nodded solemnly and held his glass out for Kirkland to top it off again.

Hell, since he came in he'd heard a dozen different accounts of the business, and every one of them had been wilder than the one before. First they said the fellow was armed. Then somebody, it might have been Cory Braxton, said he was sure the fellow'd been carrying a revolver in his pocket. Now he was supposed to have a rifle too.

Whelan shook his head in disbelief. By morning the poor SOB likely would be reported to have a Gatling gun strapped to his back. There was no telling what of it was true and what wasn't.

Still, there was no doubt that old Harry was dead. That much they'd been able to see for themselves.

Funny, though, Whelan reflected, how everyone was so het up about Harry now that the man was dead. A dozen hours ago there hadn't been a one of them that had any use for the sonofabitch. Now that he was dead and laid out in a box he was fast approaching sainthood. If Harry'd died of a heart attack, the only interest in it would have been the speculation about how much money he'd left behind and the likely run for the widow if the amount got high enough.

Whelan smiled to himself and took another drink. The guessing and the dancing around the widow would come. But first there was this other business to take care of.

Kirkland had wandered back into the crowd, taking his bottle with him. Whelan grunted and lifted his long, slightly bowed legs to prop them on the empty seat of the chair opposite him.

Across the room Colonel McKenzie—who was no kin to the famous Ranald McKenzie but who sure hated to be penned into admitting that—was giving loud instructions and laying complex plans. Practically no one was listening to him, but either he didn't realize that or was pretending that he didn't.

There was an outburst of merriment when Bert Corailis accidentally kicked over a cuspidor and spilled its contents onto Hy Rice's boots.

Then Luke Rice took offense on his brother's behalf and allowed that he was going to give Corailis a thrashing. A couple fellows grabbed Luke from behind and hauled him outside so he could cool down or throw up or whatever.

Hell of a party, Whelan thought. Probably if anybody'd guessed how much fun it would be when old Harry died, someone would have killed him a long time ago.

* * *

Whelan unhooked his boot heels from the chair seat and stood. His head felt light and swimming. He'd had more to drink than he realized, and he was beginning to feel the effects now.

And at that he was in a lot better shape than most of the boys tonight. He grinned as his cheeks puffed out from a rye-flavored burp.

Someone handed him a bottle, and he drank from it.

Justice, he thought.

Yessir, there's nothing like justice.

He was not so drunk that the irony of that stray thought missed him.

Feeling suddenly more sober, he turned and glided the hell out of there in that loose, easy, predator's gait he had.

Chapter 4

Whelan sat on the back of the tough blue roan that he had come to think of as his traveling horse—not worth a damn for real work but hell for tough on a big circle or a fast trip—and let his reins drop. He rested his hands one atop the other on the saddle horn and surveyed the scene before him with considerable amusement.

Brave words last night. Mighty little action this morning.

Dawn, they'd all said. Pull out at first light all full of snot and fury. Sure. Dawn was several hours already past and most of the boys were still moving on shaky legs, placing their feet careful and walking like they were on jointed stilts.

The only one who didn't look hung over fit to beat the hound was Colonel McKenzie. The colonel, who had once commanded a territorial militia in New Mexico, was setting his elderly bay gelding with style; the old horse patient and the old Colonel straight-backed and severe looking, chewing on his mustache and now and then barking orders that no one listened to.

The Rice boys apparently were using this jaunt into the mountains as a way to school a couple young horses. Both ponies looked green as grass, jumping and skittering and threatening to booger every time somebody came near them. Hy's still was in a bosal. At least Luke's had graduated to a snaffle bit. If the trails got bad and the going rugged, the Rices could be in a hell of a fix up there. But it was their business, of course. They were old enough; they ought to know what they wanted to do, Whelan observed without comment.

Bert Corailis, clumsy even when he was trying to be graceful, was all thumbs when he was hung over. He was trying to get his cinches tight, and his rump-spotted Nez Perce kept jumping away from him every time Bert made a stab for the keeper bar. The two of them, man and horse, were waltzing in a slow circle around and around. It would have gone easier for Bert if he'd tied the damn horse to a pen rail but he never thought of that and no one else wanted to tell him because it was so fun to watch.

Some of them were commencing to sort themselves out, though, strapping saddlebags behind their cantles and shoving carbines into the leather boots slung from their D Rings.

Whelan took a look overhead. The sun was breaking the canyon rim. Nine o'clock, he judged, or close to it. Helluva good time to start.

Kirkland sidled up next to him on a bored paint that looked about as sleepy-eyed this morning as Lou did. As soon as Lou let off the horse's bit it dropped its head and fluttered its nostrils in a disgusted blow.

"Thought you weren't coming," Lou said. He began to root around in his coat pockets but couldn't seem to find whatever it was he was looking for.

"I never said that," Whelan told him. He shrugged. "Got nothing better to do."

Which was true enough as far as it went. What stock had been up in the high country had already been brought down for the winter and all the late-borns and spring misses worked. Everybody's remudas had been turned out to grass already, and the young stuff wouldn't want working until spring. This was a fat time of year when nearly everybody could lie back and take it easy for a bit, until the hard snows came and they had to start hauling feed.

The rest of the truth was that Whelan did not want to get any of his neighbors mad at him.

He was trying to make a start on an outfit of his own after years of collecting wages, but he only had a handful of good heifers to build on and no beeves or even calves to market as yet. He was still depending on day wages to make out, and he would need the day work come the feeding season. McKenzie and Dan Troupe in particular he couldn't afford to offend. Not for a few more years, he couldn't. So it was better to ride along with the crowd.

Besides, he truly hadn't anything better to do.

"Well, I'm glad to see you're along," Lou said. He quit rummaging for whatever it was he wanted out of his pockets and twisted around to open the right flap of his bags and pull a bottle out. He offered it first to Whelan. "Something to take the hair off your tongue?"

Whelan shook his head. "My gut's still sour enough from last night."

"My point exactly. This's what you need to sweeten it." He took a short swallow and shuddered, his face twisting like he'd just gotten a dose of strong medicine.

Whelan grinned at him. "Looks like that chunk had a bone in it."

Kirkland shuddered again, took a smaller sip that seemed to satisfy more, and seated the cork with a stab of the heel of his palm. He returned the bottle to his saddlebag.

There was a flurry of excitement on the far side of the pens, and somebody came running up from the direction of the creek. It was the oldest Walters boy, fifteen or thereabouts and usually bent on acting like a grown man. Right now, though, he was shouting and waving his arms and forgetting that he was too old for such childish activity.

"He's still on that ledge," the Walters boy was shouting. "We got 'im trapped on the ledge. He's still there. We got 'im now." The boy had a .22 rifle in one hand and was threatening half the population of the county every time he waved that arm. Whelan hoped to hell the kid didn't have a round in the chamber or he was apt to put a grave next to Harry's.

"Follow me," Colonel McKenzie bellowed. "Men. Follow me."

Whelan almost laughed. Damned if the old man didn't pull a saber, an actual, honest-to-God saber, out of a scabbard hung on a ring on his hornless McClellan, and gesture with it like he was rallying a regiment, banners and all.

Most of the boys were already moving, even before the colonel shouted his orders.

Men who a moment before had been wobbling around looking like they couldn't decide whether to puke or fall down were moving fast now, swinging into their saddles, and spurring for the creek. It turned into a regular horse race, and in seconds there wasn't anything but dust left in the stage-station yard.

Kirkland went whooping along with the rest of them. Whelan hung back, letting the crowd sort itself out for a bit, then bumped the roan into a lope and trailed after them.

It wasn't like they were going far. The creek was only a couple hundred yards away and past that there was just the canyon wall that the city fellow had somehow climbed yesterday.

Whelan stopped when he cleared the line of trees at the edge of the flat, rocky flood plain by the creek. He took a look at the canyon wall where Harry's killer was holed up.

It was a helluva climb the man had made. Whelan had to give him credit for that. It wasn't a thing Tom would have wanted to try. The face was nearly sheer and the rock crumbly, the kind of thing that even a cat or a mountain goat would think twice about before tackling. Yet the guy had got up it.

Partway anyhow.

Everybody was peering and pointing toward a ledge about three-quarters of the way up the face, those who couldn't spot it being helped by the Walters boys and their father and uncles, who had stayed the night by the creek to guard against the guy coming down unobserved.

The sun was angled so that once you spotted the ledge you couldn't see how you ever missed it the first time, although that was actually pretty easy—missing it, that is—with bright sunlight and harsh shadow turning the whole top half of the cliff face into a patchwork of light and dark that at first seemed to have no depth to it.

The colonel was gesturing men into position with the blade of his saber, and this time the boys were more or less obeying him. They were forming into a line along the creek, everybody with rifles or carbines in their hands now and staring up toward the ledge.

Whelan stepped his roan forward a few paces so he could see better, then let his reins drop and hooked a knee over his horn. He pulled the makings out of his pocket and began to build a smoke.

Kirkland came racing back toward him, his horse splashing cold water onto a couple of the boys as Lou charged back across the creek. "Hurry, Tom. We got him cornered up there. Gonna lay a volley onto the overhang 'bove that ledge and drive him out with the ricochets." Kirkland looked as excited as a kid with new spurs.

"They don't need me for that, Lou. You sure he's up there? I sure don't see any sign of smoke this morning. Didn't somebody say he'd built him a fire when he got up there last night?"

"He's tryin' to pretend he ain't there. But Ned Walters says him and his boys all seen movement just a minute ago. Like as if the guy was sneaking a peek down to see what we're up to, you know?"

"Could be then." Whelan gave his quirrly a final twist and a lick, then struck a match to the tip of it. The extra paper at the end flared and a few flakes of burning tobacco drifted down onto his vest until the rest of it caught properly and formed a coal. The smoke tasted good.

"You aren't gonna shoot?"

"Sure. Soon as I see something to shoot at. You boys go ahead an' have your fun."

"Well I ain't gonna be left out." Kirkland wheeled his horse and splashed back across the creek, drawing another round of curses from the men he bathed in the icy water.

The colonel had everybody lined up now and rifles aimed. There wasn't much of an overhang for them to shoot into, but with so many bullets flying they surely all couldn't miss. Whelan sat where he was, Marlin repeater still in its boot, and paid attention to the ledge instead of the men.

With all that lead splattering, anything on the ledge was sure to be flushed.

"Fire!" McKenzie barked in a parade-ground voice.

There was a long, ragged volley of gunshots that drowned the old man's voice, and an area ten feet square was churned up with rock dust and smears of bright, silvery lead high on the cliff face.

"Again, men. Give him another volley," the colonel ordered, and the volunteers complied. Not quite everybody was able to comply this time, though. The noise of that first shooting had set the Rice boys' young geldings into a fit of bucking, and roughly a third of the crowd was trying to get out of their way while another third was laughing at the first third. Luke's sorrel took a swipe at Dor Winston's pony and got kicked in return, the hooves of Dor's horse just missing Luke's leg and getting an argument started about which of them should watch what he was doing.

Those who'd gotten distracted went back to the business at hand, and any accidental semblance of order in the volleying dissolved into random shooting, everybody firing toward the ledge as quick as he could throw a lever and yank a trigger.

Chips and dust rained down the ledge with a will now, and some of the bigger pieces dislodged others until there was a small rock slide going.

Even with all of that going on there was no sign of anything moving. Whelan thought once he might have seen a hint of motion inside one of the cracks off to the right of the ledge. A chipmunk, probably, or maybe a cony or small bird. For damn sure no man was hiding inside a crack that looked to be three or four inches wide.

But that was all the movement Whelan saw.

He grunted to himself and dropped his leg off the horn, finding the stirrup with his toe and righting himself in the saddle.

Likely it was some small something like that that had

caused the movement the Walters boys saw this morning. Likely Harry's murderer was long gone.

Not that Whelan expected to convince anybody else of that.

He sighed. What this was going to do, of course, was just delay them getting off. Give the guy that much more time to move along.

He wasn't likely to get away, though. Not in the long run.

There just wasn't any place for the guy to run to. Not for seventy, eighty miles over into Idaho. And that was if you knew where you were going and how you get there.

Whelan didn't think this man would know. The boys who had actually been there when the guy killed Harry said he was dressed like a dude. Not slick like a Missouri gambler but citified. Low shoes and necktie. Pale like he worked indoors. Hair slicked flat and parted down the middle. Not the sort, they all said, who you'd expect to up and murder a man for no reason. Yet he'd done it.

In over his head now, though, Whelan thought, unless he was some kind of bad hombre just out of prison and pale from that. That was a thought. It was possible.

Still, unless he was awfully good in rough country, he'd got his tail in the crack now.

There wasn't anything ahead of him but raw mountains and deep canyons.

And the boys who were hunting him knew those mountains from running cattle in them every summer.

In the long run the killer was just plain done for.

The question wasn't whether they would catch him but how long it would take.

The colonel was trying to get everybody to quit shooting now, but that was turning out to be a chore. A few of them seemed to think that the shooting was about as much fun as fireworks on the Fourth, and they weren't ready to quit.

While that was going on, the oldest Walters boy and his just-younger brother were peeling off their coats and moving over toward the place where the killer had started up the cliff. Whelan guessed that they were being sent up to see if the guy had been killed on the ledge.

That would mean another hour or more before the colonel's posse got under way.

Whelan stepped down and loosened his cinches. No point in making the roan pay for the delay. He tossed the butt of his smoke away, long habit making him extinguish the coal first even though there was nothing to burn on the gravel of the flood plain where he stood.

"I think we got him," somebody said as the Walters boys started their climb.

Chapter 5

Drayne huddled in a niche of rock, arms wrapped tight against his chest, still shivering a little. At least the sun's heat was finally beginning to warm him. It was a relief after the miserable night he had just spent.

He had wakened sometime in the night when it was still much too dark to bother trying to see his watch. It was the cold that woke him. His fire had died, and even if he could have started it again, it would only have served to pinpoint him for the marksmen he expected would still be down below.

He tried moving about to warm himself, but the ledge was too small to permit much in the way of motion. A misstep would have sent him plummeting to the canyon floor.

So he did the next best thing. At least it had seemed the best course at the time.

Now, shuddering as he remembered it, he was not so sure.

He climbed on, finding hand- and footholds by feel in the darkness, at first grateful for the warmth the exercise gave him, then, when it was too late to turn back, terrified of the danger of his predicament.

Three, four times he had slipped when a handhold gave way and he very nearly fell, catching and righting himself by luck rather than skill.

It was probably just as well that he was not able to see the cliff face he was climbing. If he had, he might not have been able to force himself to do it.

That was behind him now, though, thank God.

He finally reached the top and set out at a swift walk in an effort both to escape and keep warm. That had been miles back. How many miles he had no way to tell. He was more accustomed to dealing in city blocks than in miles. How many blocks in a mile? He couldn't remember. If he had ever known.

At least now the sun was warming him. And for the first time he was conscious of hunger. Surely that was a good sign. He would consider it so even if it was not. A small success to bolster hope.

He had survived the climb. Survived the cold of the night. Survived those first miles of flight.

That was good.

And anything that was good he would cling to.

He relaxed his arms from around his own thin chest, shivered a bit in protest and then basked in the warm sunlight that flooded the tiny pocket of rock where he had stopped to rest.

Plans. He had to plan ahead. If he expected to continue to survive, he had to come up with a plan of survival.

Take stock. Plan for what was possible. Consider contingencies. Alternatives. That was good advice in this forsaken wilderness just as it would be in business dealings.

Think, he told himself firmly.

He was young. Healthy. Reasonably bright. Reasonably fit, everything considered.

Hungry, of course. And his hands hurt. They were stiffening again. But that was nothing debilitating. His feet and legs were still in fine shape.

He needed food and either clothing or shelter. For the moment there was nothing to be done about that. Nothing that he could think of or knew how to accomplish. A woodsman might know how to cope. Bryan Drayne did not.

The point now, though, was not to concentrate on the negatives but on the positive aspects of this miserable situation.

Point. He had to escape from the fools who were bent on exacting vengeance for Harry's accidental death.

Option? He could give himself up to them? Explain? Expect understanding?

No, he judged. Not that. They already tried to shoot him. They were not amenable to reason. He might consider surrender to a proper officer of the law but not to these men. He had read too much about vigilance-committee justice in this part of the country.

He had to run at least until he could find a rational, impartial officer of the law who would listen to his side of the story and seek justice for him in a court of law.

All right then. Run. But where?

Where, indeed? He hadn't even much of an idea of where he *was* much less where he wanted to go.

Somewhere near the Montana-Idaho border. He believed he had heard the coach driver say that they would be in Idaho by the next changing of the team.

Did that present hope? There would be different legal jurisdiction upon crossing state lines—except there was no legal jurisdiction to hold a mob in check. No benefit there, then.

Except that an Idaho law officer would be less inclined to emotional responses about a crime committed in Montana.

Crime, he reflected. Had he committed a crime? Was he in fact now a criminal?

Irrelevant, he chided himself.

What mattered at the moment was not what he *was* but what those possemen *perceived* him to be. That was what mattered now. The rest could be attended to later. After he successfully escaped.

He needed to move westward. Into Idaho. Find an officer of the law. Receive protection from the law from these men; hire an attorney.

He glanced up toward the sun, trying to get a sense of direction, then to the west and again to the north. The road the stage followed headed west. The route was to have been Great Falls, Helena, Coeur d'Alene and beyond. So logically the stage road tended westward. He had paid no attention to the specifics of the road. When they stopped to eat and change horses, the road had been at the bottom of the canyon. Presumably, it rose into the mountains somewhere north of the way station Harry managed and turned westward somewhere.

He reached for his pipe, remembering too late that his coat, pipe, and tobacco pouch were still back at that godforsaken stage station.

It was only dumb luck that he had a nearly full box of matches in his trousers pocket when he fled the place. He stood, actually feeling quite comfortable now in the sunshine, and looked down and examined his own clothing.

He was wearing a shirt of good quality and tailoring. White, though, which could be seen from a distance. A necktie. Collar and cuff buttons. Celluloid collar now somewhat limp. Suspenders. Shoes nearly new, with good laces. Stockings and stocking garters. Trousers of a weight suitable for fall wear.

He grunted once and went through his pockets.

He had his watch with short chain and a penknife instead of a fob. The knife could be invaluable. It had a single blade, only an inch or so long but sturdy. Not particularly sharp but certainly of potential benefit. Loose pocket change in the amount of $17.60. His wallet containing his paper money was in the inside pocket of his coat, wherever that was now. Not that there was anyplace here to spend money no matter how much he had.

He went through the rest of his pockets.

A clean handkerchief neatly folded. Keys to his house and office. So distant. So useless. Separate keys to his trunk, still loaded somewhere on the coach.

The box of matches. He slid it open and counted. He had twenty-three matches in the container. No problem there. He would not be wasting any on lighting his pipe, although at this moment he would have given nearly anything for the comfort of a pipe. Right now he thought he missed the pipe more than he did food.

He returned the matches to his pocket, wound his watch, and became conscious again of how stiff his fingers had become.

Somewhere off to the east he could hear a low, dull roar of distant thunder although there were no clouds that appeared threatening.

Drayne frowned. He suspected the sound had meaning. It was man-made. But the sound and its meaning escaped him.

He looked toward the sun again to be sure of his directions, then turned and began trudging toward distant peaks that jutted skyward with awesome menace.

He walked, ignoring the pangs of hunger that now and then clenched and churned in his stomach.

Behind him the thunderlike sounds continued, although now with less intensity. The dull, distant reports came from the direction of the canyon he had just escaped.

But he was not thinking about that now. He was refusing to dwell on the negative. He was planning toward the future now. That was much easier to cope with than the reactions of terror.

Bryan Drayne was no longer terrified. He was, in fact, no longer particularly afraid.

Chapter 6

The fear returned that afternoon. Not consuming fear. There was no panic in him now. But there was a cold thrill of fear that pulled him to a halt, as he peered off to the east—back the way he had just come.

Dogs. Somewhere behind he was almost sure he had just heard the baying of dogs.

They were chasing him with dogs.

Chasing? Or tracking?

It hardly seemed to matter at the moment.

"Damn," he muttered aloud, the sound of it in the uncomfortable, unnatural silence startling him for a moment.

Dogs.

He had begun to hope that he had eluded them. That all he had to do now was walk out of this wilderness, to travel overland sufficiently far that he could find a road, follow it to civilization, and resume his journey to Seattle.

"Damn," he said again.

He had begun to hope that the nightmare of Harry and the vigilantes was behind him. That he could simply go on and pretend nothing happened. Disappear in the west. Make his way to Seattle. Wire home for a letter of credit to replace the funds lost at that way station and go on as if nothing had ever happened.

Drayne shuddered. He would not be so lucky.

He had seen packs of dogs before. Hounds on a fox hunt when he was in Virginia on a business trip. That well-remembered scene had been a gala for the people involved. Whiskey and wine and handsome women mounted on tall horses. The natives had been quite charming, actually. The whole thing had been a gay, festive occasion for them.

Unused to such things as hunting and hounds, Drayne had thought it crude, even cruel. Bloodily messy at the end. And his host had insisted that he be in on the end of it, the overweight and aging host following behind the baying of the vicious pack of beasts at a distance. Drayne rode beside him on the upholstered seat of the swaying, lurching coach while the driver tried to maintain voice contact with the pack.

It had not been a pleasant experience, and the worst of it had been when they reached the final covert, the leader of the hunt—what the *hell* had they titled him?—waiting for the arrival of the host, the dogs a churning, unruly mob and the handsome men and women now disheveled and sitting nervous, sweat-lathered horses.

Drayne shuddered again, remembering the savagery. The old man struggling—grinning, upright in the bed of the phaeton—to give a nod to the kill. The release of the dogs. The viciousness of that final attack, all snarls and growls and slashing teeth.

The dogs had dragged the small red fox from its hole, and literally tore the smaller animal apart with unimaginable fury.

The fool huntsmen had been proud of themselves, and pleased with the performance of their horses, their dogs, and even of the fox itself. Over and over he had heard people speaking fondly of the fox, by then reduced to bloody tatters of red fur and scraps of naked skin. The entire episode had sickened Drayne.

And now his stomach churned as he heard the distant cry of a dog tracking his scent. His trail. This time Drayne was the one the dogs would bring to bay, and he broke into a sweat as he saw himself being torn apart by the hungry dogs.

Involuntarily he pressed his palms against his belly to protect himself from the assault, and shivered, suddenly cold again. When another hound's voice rose through the wilderness, Drayne turned west and began to run blindly from the threat of the pack.

Chapter 7

Whelan hung back at the rear of the posse. There was finally a sense of excitement among the men after the frustrations of the morning, and Feeney was gloating at being the center of attention now that his dogs had the scent.

Had *a* scent, Whelan corrected himself. They might or might not be following the man who had killed Harry. As far as Whelan could remember, the only things Feeney's pack had hunted were bears and the odd cat. They had never been asked to track a man before and might or might not be up to the task.

Be a helluva thing, Whelan thought, if all of this was in pursuit of a mountain lion or a grizzly. Wouldn't that put a crimp in the party?

No one else seemed to be worried about the possibility though.

Men who had been riding all morning with their Winchesters slung on their saddles now were pulling the stubby, slab-sided carbines from their scabbards and cranking cartridges into chambers that should have been empty.

Hell's bells, there was no telling how old the trail was, even if it was the man they were on to and not some animal.

Whelan rode loose and easy behind them, feeling more an observer than a participant. Certainly he felt none of the excitement that was gripping the rest of the posse and pulling their faces into the hard grins they flashed at one another.

He left his Marlin hanging in the boot under his right leg.

Up front he could see the two men who were sharing the lead of the posse. Quite a contrast between them too, he thought.

Colonel McKenzie was riding upright in his saddle, rigid as the sword blade he carried low by his thigh. The old man was riding chin high and proud. He had a command again, ragtag and scruffy though it might be, and Whelan could see the pride in him just from the way he carried himself. Even the old gelding seemed to've picked up on it and was moving at an alert, high-stepping gait that would have looked fine in a parade-ground review.

Beside him Bill Feeney was about as different from the colonel as any man could get.

Whelan didn't know Feeney all that well. The man tended to stay pretty much to himself, making a meager living off bounty money he received for the wolf and coyote scalps his traps brought in. Now and then he would show up among folks to throw a drunk and then crawl back to the solitary canyon where he kept to himself.

Feeney was as tall as the colonel and as thin. *Scrawny* described him better. Whelan had never seen him when he hadn't needed a shave, although for some reason he never quite grew a beard. His hair was dark but thinning, and he had a mouthful of gaps where teeth should have been.

The man rode a horse that was so bony it looked like it wouldn't make it through another winter. But it had looked the same last fall and the year before that, and it always seemed to manage to survive, like its owner did.

Feeney's saddle and clothes looked as poor as his horse. He rode in a slouch, leaning forward now and then to curse at his dogs and bawl out names. "Jessie! Little Red! Git on, damn you, git on."

Those dogs were Feeney's only companions; he made his living, such as it was, from them, but if he felt any affection for them, Whelan had never seen a hint of it. Feeney was equally sour with man and beast and showed neither humor nor gentleness in any form. Whelan had never particularly thought about it before, but he did not much like the man. Feeney seemed to be riding high now, though. Now that nearly the whole valley was following his lead in the chase after Harry's murderer.

The posse was moving at an easy jog. The dogs were slow trailers, mixed breeds trained to push the quarry just hard enough to bring it to tree.

Just then they came to a stop as the dogs slowed and milled in front of them, snarling and snapping at each other. The men waited while Feeney rode into the middle of the pack, slashing down at the dogs with an overlong quirt while he cussed and threatened them. "Git on, damn you. Seek. Seek."

"What's the matter, Bill?"

Feeney shrugged. "Guy stopped here to take a piss. Somethin'. I don't know." He leaned down and with the quirt viciously slashed the back of his pack leader's head, bringing a howl of protest from the startled dog, who bolted with his tail between his legs.

"Git on, Josie," Feeney snapped.

Josie took up the scent again, and Feeney quirted the pack apart. The dogs yapped uncertainly for a moment, then set out in pursuit of Josie. The pack leader was racing ahead now, and the others ran to catch up. They did not lower their muzzles to the scent and begin to bell again until they were close behind Josie.

"Forward, men," McKenzie ordered unnecessarily as the posse spurred to follow the dogs. Feeney was already loping ahead, and the rest of them were moving with him.

Luke Rice ended up riding beside Whelan. He tossed a grin Whelan's way and asked, "What d'you think, Tom?"

Whelan shrugged. "I think we don't have him yet."

"Got to be close though, right?"

"Do you see him?"

Rice seemed to take the question seriously. He stood in his stirrups to stare forward, beyond the pack of tracking dogs, then shook his head. "Not yet," he said.

"Then we don't know how close we are, do we?"

"The guy sure has covered a lotta ground," Luke said

with a hint of complaint in his voice. "City fella too. He sure has covered a lotta ground."

"You never know about a man from looking at him," Whelan observed. "I saw Corbett once."

"Gentleman Jim? For real?" Rice sounded impressed. "You never told me that."

Whelan shrugged. "It was down in Butte one time. Though he wasn't fighting there or nothing. He was just having his supper at the hotel. Fella I was with pointed him out to me or I'd never have known who he was. Looked like a banker or a stockbroker or something in a bat-wing and tie. Looked like a regular dude, he did. And this is a man that used to be the heavyweight champion of the whole world."

"Did you go over an' talk to him?" Luke asked excitedly.

"Hell no, I didn't go bother the man. And that ain't the point. The point is that Corbett was as tough a man as I've ever laid eyes on, but he sure as hell didn't look anything special. I wouldn't have thought a thing about him, nor would've hesitated to get into a brawl with him, if I hadn't been told who he was. That's the point I'm making here."

"You mean this could be one bad sonofabitch we're after?"

"I'm just saying we don't really know anything about him. Me, I don't figure to assume he's good or bad or anything else until I *know* what he is."

Rice looked serious and took a firmer grip on the wrist of the Winchester '92 he was carrying in his right hand. "They say he's heavy armed."

"No," Whelan said. "The guy might or might not be carrying a pistol, but he isn't heavy armed. Scared, prob'ly. On the run for sure. But he's trying to get away from us, not stand and fight."

Rice nodded and looked relieved about that reminder. After all, it was the posse that was in control here and doing the chasing, not the murderer. The murderer was a city man, and he was on the run.

"You think we'll catch up with him soon?" he asked.

Whelan shrugged again. "We'll catch him when we

catch him. No way anybody can know about that till it happens."

"I'll be glad to get this done with," Luke said. He sounded grim. And perhaps worried too.

"So will I," Whelan said softly.

He eased back on his reins a fraction, slowing the roan just a bit so that Luke Rice drifted ahead and Whelan was able to resume his position alone at the back of the crowd.

They were moving at a jog again as Feeney's dogs belled and hunted, forging ahead at a steady clip.

Whelan reached into his shirt pocket for his tobacco makings, dropping his reins behind the horn and guiding the roan with his knees so he could use both hands for the task. He was not surprised that they had not yet caught up with the city man. They had given him a good lead with the slow start and shenanigans of the morning. But a man who was unfamiliar with this country could not stay ahead of them very much longer. Not if it was his scent the dogs were trailing. They would catch up with him before too much longer.

He rolled his smoke, cupped his hands to shield the match flame, and settled in to ride loose and easy in his saddle while the others hung on to their weapons like they expected Harry's murderer to try to ambush them at any moment.

Tom Whelan felt no such expectation. But if it happened, he would be more ready for it than any of the rest of them, gun in hand or not. That, at least, he could feel sure of.

He broke his match and made sure it was out before he dropped it and picked up his reins again, clucking softly to the blue roan and increasing its gait a bit as he eased nearer to the back of the posse.

Chapter 8

"That sonofabitch," Dor Winston said with considerable feeling. "That miserable, low, no-account sonofabitch."

The posse was stopped at the rim of a narrow gulch. The dogs were thirty or forty feet down the wall of the cut, stopped cold on an outcrop of gray rock and unable to go any further. The horsebackers, uncertain of their footing on the loose gravel, were unable to ride down even that far.

"Sonofabitch," someone else repeated. Whelan couldn't decide if the voice was just cussing in general or aiming it at the murderer in particular.

"He can't outrun us," Whelan said. "So he's trying to out maneuver us. Makes sense."

"The sonofabitch," Dor said again.

Whelan stepped down off his saddle and loosened his cinches. If they were going to fool around here grumbling and complaining, he might as well use the time to give the roan a blow.

Lou Kirkland noticed what Tom was doing and dismounted. "What d'you think, Tom?"

Whelan glanced at the sky, where the sun was well into its descent on the western horizon. "What I think is that we aren't gonna catch up to him before dark, that's what I think."

"I was sure hoping to get home tonight," Kirkland said.

Whelan shrugged.

"Gather around, men," Colonel McKenzie said in a loud voice. "Gather around."

Slowly, the possemen gathered close around the

colonel's saddle skirts and gave their attention to the old militia commander. Feeney had been busy trying to call his dogs back up onto the rim, but even he stopped and listened now.

"Here is our situation," the colonel said. "The killer is attempting to use the terrain against us."

Whelan kept a straight face but couldn't help thinking that Colonel McKenzie was about the only man he'd ever come across who could use a word like *terrain* in a conversation and make it sound like it belonged.

"The killer obviously knows that we are tracking him with dogs, and he is attempting to use that knowledge to his advantage. He wishes to turn our dependence on dogs and horses to his own advantage by leading us into terrain where neither horses nor dogs can follow."

That was as plain as the palm of a man's roping hand, as the colonel laid it out for them, but some of the boys were nodding their heads, all solemn and serious, like they were getting official word from on high.

"We will envelop the killer in a classic pincer movement," the colonel said, whatever the hell that was supposed to mean, and again most of the boys nodded their agreement. Just like they understood everything.

"Winston, you are perhaps the man most familiar with this country," McKenzie boomed in his parade-ground voice.

"I'd say so," Dor agreed. He and his partner John Archer ran stock in the area every summer. "I got a line cabin at the head of this canyon, and we built some stock ponds down-canyon."

McKenzie rubbed the hilt of his scabbarded saber in contemplation at that reminder. "The killer could well wish to hole up in your cabin. We might capture him there." The colonel grunted softly, as if to himself, and cleared his throat. "In view of that information, gentlemen, I suggest we postpone our pincer operation and launch an assault instead on the, uh, line shack."

"What if he ain't there?" someone asked.

"Or what if he just plain missed it?" Winston put in. "It ain't all that easy to spot if you don't know what you're looking for. Just an old dugout. There's lots o' dugouts and shacks around, what with the prospectors years back an' now the cow camps. He could walk right past the place an' not know he'd missed it."

"Logically," the colonel said, "the killer will be seeking shelter and sustenance. A line camp is the most logical source of either. First we investigate the one shelter we know of in this vicinity. Then if necessary we resume operations. What is the quickest route to this gulch, Winston?"

Dor thought this over for a minute, taking a look around to orient himself, then pointed south. "Down there. Gotta go all the way to the mouth to get down, I'd say. There's no path, exactly, but I expect we can get down if we don't mind some rump sliding."

"Nothing closer? At the head of the gulch perhaps?"

"Nothing that way but bare rock and a helluva cliff. I doubt that a chipmunk could get down up-canyon."

McKenzie nodded, then turned to Feeney and said, "Collect your hounds, man."

"I been tryin', dammit," Feeney snapped back at him.

The colonel stiffened in his saddle, although Whelan would have thought that the old man was already sitting about as stiff-backed as a human person could get.

Feeney saw and gestured with open palms to show that he hadn't meant anything personal with his tone of voice. It occurred to Whelan that Bill Feeney was probably dependent on McKenzie for some of his coyote-scalp money just like Whelan needed the winter day wages the colonel could pay.

"I just meant it'll take me a few minutes, that's all."

McKenzie nodded coldly as Feeney dismounted and started scrambling down the slope to the dogs.

Alonso Cantwell dismounted and handed his reins to Winston, then scrambled down the slippery slope to help Feeney. Between them they managed to drive the dogs off the scent and send them hustling back up to the rim with their tails low and teeth bared. Feeney's pack was no bunch of play-pets for children to mess with, that was for sure.

Even with the two men down there and the crowd on

top to call and whistle and try to encourage the dogs, the job took some time.

They hadn't all that much daylight left to play with, Whelan noticed. Damn the late start they had gotten.

"Right, men," the colonel announced when they were finally set. "Follow me."

He rode south along the rim of the gulch, just as upright and stiff as he had been when they started. Feeney and his dogs followed at the rear this time, and Dor Winston rode forward with McKenzie.

Even without trying to tackle that steep-walled slope down into the canyon, there were some places where the horses had to scramble to make it over the rocks and through dense clumps of juniper. The footing was bad and the going slow, and Whelan resigned himself to at least one more day with the posse.

It was the better part of three rough miles to a place where Winston said he thought they could get down into the gulch. And that spot wasn't much account.

Everybody dismounted and checked their cinches before they tackled it, and when they started down, the Rice boys held back until the last and then came down afoot, not trusting their green horses to make it without boogering or starting some sort of commotion. It was just as well that they did. The dogs were the only creatures, human or otherwise, who made it down comfortably.

Thinking he might have to make a fast get-off, Whelan slipped his boots back in his stirrups until he had only toe contact, leaned far back over his cantle and gave the roan its head. The horse hadn't much cow sense, but it wasn't stupid, and it was as tough as any animal he'd ever ridden. He made it to the bottom with only some minor slipping and sliding, but even so was relieved that the gulch wasn't any deeper than it was.

Each horse started a small avalanche of pea gravel, and Corailis's animal took a fall that could have been nasty, although it turned out that man and horse came through more scared than hurt.

The Rice boys let their horses come down empty, Luke and Hy followed behind on a slope so steep they had to come down on their butts. The young horses weren't spooky about people, fortunately, and allowed themselves to be caught once they were on level ground again.

Whelan took hold of the reins of Luke's sorrel and returned the animal to him.

"Thanks."

Whelan nodded. He was paying attention to McKenzie, who was looking about like he was surprised how shadowy it was down here at the bottom of the cut.

The gulch walls were steep on both sides, and direct sunlight probably only reached the floor at midday.

"Mount up now. We've no time to waste," the colonel ordered.

The old man pretended not to notice that nearly everyone rode over to let their mounts at the water in one of the stock ponds Winston and Archer had developed near the mouth of the gulch. The horses drank their fill and then they were all ready again.

"Carefully now," McKenzie warned. "The killer may be armed and dangerous."

They were still a long way from Winston's line shack, but even so most of the boys pulled their Winchesters again and began to look nervous.

McKenzie drew his sword and held it at attention or present arms or something—Whelan had no idea what the formal posture should be called—but the hilt was held stiffly low at his side with the blade upright and locked tight against his shoulder. It looked impressive, whatever the colonel might have called it.

"For-ward . . . march."

Nobody seemed to think the command silly under the circumstances.

They rode up-canyon at a lope, McKenzie leading and the rest of the boys trailing behind in a loose formation with Bill Feeney and his dogs at the end of the ragged column.

Whelan glanced up when they passed under the spot where he thought they had lost the trail on the rim. The dogs looked like they were interested in taking up the scent again, but Feeney quirted them out of the notion.

Whelan shook his head. What little daylight they had left was being wasted. If the murderer had wanted to go up canyon, he most likely would have gone that way without crossing the creek. The dogs were acting like they had crossed a scent back there and then lost it. No one else seemed to be paying any attention, including Feeney, and they continued on behind the colonel's lead. Most likely, though, the murderer hadn't just used the gulch wall to lose the dogs once; he'd run straight across and up the west wall so he could do it again there. Still, there wouldn't be any harm in checking the dugout, just in case the man had doubled back. Besides, late as it was, they would be wanting a place to spend the night soon. The line camp would be as good a place as any and better than most. With luck there would even be some food there that they could use to extend their supplies. Whelan suspected that some of the boys had come on this hunt better prepared to drink than to eat, so extra food off Winston's shelves would be a help.

Whelan glanced once over his left shoulder before they followed a bend out of sight of the place. There was no sign of the murderer up there. Not that he had really expected any.

Tomorrow they were going to have to get serious about this chase and get it over with.

Chapter 9

Lordy, but that had been close. Drayne lay under the needled green overhang of a small tree and tried to catch his breath after the climb.

If the dogs had come on him just then, there would have been nothing he could do to defend himself. He was exhausted, lungs heaving and heart hammering.

But the dogs were several hundred yards away, on the opposite side of the canyon, at the top of the cliff where he had stopped them. His plan had worked.

The men could follow, of course. Anywhere Drayne could run a man could follow. There was nothing he could do about that. He was hoping, though, that they would continue to depend on the dogs and horses as they pursued him.

That was his only advantage over them. A man could climb places where dogs and horses could not follow.

So long as he was lucky enough to find such places.

He shuddered. The chill in his spine had nothing to do with temperature, although it seemed to be dropping now that he was out of the sun.

He could see the men now too. Up on top of the far rim, above where the dogs had been stopped by the cliff.

There looked to be an awful lot of men in the posse. They kept moving back and forth, shielded behind trees, so he was not sure how many there were.

Not that it really mattered. One was all it would take. One man with a gun in his hand could kill him.

He had to lose all of them. Easier said than done. Especially in this strange, empty wilderness that was so completely foreign to anything he had ever experienced before.

For a moment he inwardly cursed himself for his foolishness in deciding to take a coach west. The railroad . . . He shook himself. No amount of wishful ness would help him now. He could not afford to dwell on things that had not happened. Only on that which *was.*

He shivered, and it occurred to him that he probably could not afford to spend much more time without protection from the elements. The day had not been so bad with the sun to warm him, but he knew that the nights in these mountains were cold.

He was lying on a bed of fallen evergreen needles that helped protect him from the dropping temperatures, trapping his body heat and insulating him from the cold of the ground and of the air that chilled his back and legs. He wriggled, burrowing a little deeper into the needles, enjoying the temporary warmth.

Across the canyon he could see a tall, spare man near the rim turn in his saddle and say something to the others. After a moment the other men gathered closer around the tall one.

So that was the leader of the vigilantes, Drayne thought. That was the face of the enemy. Drayne wished he was close enough to hear what was being said.

He wished . . . He wished for quite a lot of things, actually.

Bitterly Drayne lay where he was and watched the men.

He was trapped here now. If he tried to slip away while the vigilantes were in plain sight, he was almost sure to be seen. Then the deception with the dogs would have been to no purpose.

Probably they could even shoot him from where they now stood.

Drayne had scant knowledge of how far a rifle bullet could carry. But he suspected he was well within rifle shot of the horsemen at this moment. He could see them clearly. Not well enough to make out faces or voices but close enough to see what kind of clothing they wore and what kind of weapons they carried. And close enough to see that most of them seemed to have bedrolls and bundles of supplies tied behind their saddles.

Damn them.

Drayne wished he had a weapon of his own. Not only for defense, dammit, but to shoot them down, every man and horse and dog among them. Annihilate the bastards. *Make them go away.*

Drayne squeezed his eyes tight shut and buried himself a bit deeper into the warmth of the needles.

Quit thinking about the impossible, he told himself firmly. Concentrate on the possible. Plan!

He grunted softly with wry, dry amusement.

That was easy enough, wasn't it? Escape. Run the hell away from these people.

That was all he had to do. Just get away from them and pretend that Harry and these vigilantes and their whole miserable world simply failed to exist.

Drayne shivered again.

That was all he had to do. Sure.

Across the canyon the men had quit listening to the tall, slim leader. One of them got off his horse and picked his way carefully down toward the dogs. Then another dismounted and followed.

They had come to some decision. That much was obvious. But what was it?

For a moment panic clutched at Drayne's throat and tight bands of fear gripped his chest.

Had they figured it out? Would they find a way to cross to the rim where he was hiding or would they first investigate the canyon floor?

That was the thing.

If they tried to put the dogs on him at the bottom of that far cliff now, he would gain more time on them. He would have lost the dogs for a second time at the cliff on this side.

But if they guessed what he had done, if they came straight across to this side . . .

The dogs could trail him at night.

And at night it would be almost impossible for him to find places where he could lose them. The cliffs were his only salvation. If the posse came after him in the darkness, he had no chance.

He nearly bolted out of his hiding place into a desperate run for freedom, but quickly realized they would see him.

The men were still there. Sitting on strong, swift horses and waiting while the two on foot tried to call the dogs off Drayne's scent.

Damn them. Damn them each and every one.

He groaned with relief when the two finally succeeded in kicking and whipping the dogs back onto the rim.

The vigilantes remounted and rode off toward the south, while the dogs trailed behind.

Drayne lay where he was until they were out of sight and then continued to lie there for a few minutes more, hesitant to expose himself in the event the posse had left someone behind to watch.

He should have counted them when he had the chance. Should have counted to see how many were there and how many rode south. Should have assured himself that none were left behind to shoot him in the back.

He shouldn't have been here at all. But he was.

If he lay here under the pine tree and waited for the posse, they would find him. If he moved, he had a chance, and he knew he would have to make the most of whatever chance he had.

He came to his knees, still wary of the possibility that a rifleman might be hidden on the far rim of the canyon. He could see nothing over there. But that proved nothing. He had lain here and watched and they had not seen him. One of them could be doing the same. He backed out from under the little tree, keeping its bulk between himself and that distant rim, and became aware of how cold the air felt against his chest and belly after the warmth of the needles. He began to shiver and wished he could take the damn needles with him, but . . .

Drayne stopped where he was, still on hands and knees, and thought about that.

If he could take the needles with him . . .

He rocked back onto his haunches and opened the top few buttons of his shirt.

Quickly he began to snatch up handfuls of the fallen needles and stuff them inside his shirt, stuffing himself like a sausage front and rear, trying to build a barrier that would hold and maintain his body heat.

The needles made a damned lousy coat. They scratched and poked and itched. But they did seem to help. At least a little.

He stuffed his shirt until it would hold no more, then loosened his trousers and stuffed more needles inside them. That was less successful. Loose needles sifted down his floppy trousers legs, tickling him as they fell.

Perhaps he should tie . . . better yet . . . He unsnapped his stocking garters and refastened them outside his trouser cuffs, closing the open bottoms of the pant legs, then resumed pouring the dry needles into his waistband, wiggling now and then to settle the bulky needles lower.

The thought struck him that all that bulk was probably making him look like a rag doll stuffed near to bursting with cotton puffs.

But he kept at it, stuffing his clothing until he was almost completely padded in dried needles.

He felt warmer. He itched practically everywhere but he felt genuinely warmer. And that was what he wanted.

He felt better too beyond the warmth. More competent somehow. He was actually feeling quite good then when he stood and finished buttoning and fastening his clothing again.

Somewhere the vigilantes and their dogs were continuing to ride after him. There still could be someone lying in wait on the far side of the canyon.

But Drayne felt a little better about himself now, felt a lift to his spirits that went far beyond the physical benefit of a warmer body.

Keeping the tree between himself and where a rifleman might be hidden, he began walking west. He walked awkwardly, almost waddling, as the needles irritated his crotch and thighs.

The sun ahead of him was low in the sky now,

dropping toward peaks of unimaginable height.

He wanted to find at least one more cliff face too sheer for the dogs before he rested again.

Just one.

Surely that would stop them at least until the morning.

Then with luck, tomorrow . . . he would think about that tomorrow. Now he walked uncomfortably on to the west.

Chapter 10

He woke shuddering from the deep, bone-aching cold and shuddering even more from the fear that had consumed him in the dream.

Dogs. Fangs. Slavering, slobbering jaws gaping wide. Dogs.

He sat upright and listened, still shivering and shaking from the combination of nightmare-induced terror and extreme cold.

He knew it had been a dream. But he had to listen, to convince himself that he had not heard the baying of dogs coming after him.

There was no sound in the night but the soft whisper of a predawn breeze seeping through the needles of the evergreens nearby.

He had slept . . . he was not sure how long, but it could have been no more than an hour or two. Certainly it had been for very little time. There was no hint of dawn in the sky in the east, and the cold was reaching through the brittle, breaking needles packed around his body. Their protection was better than nothing but far from enough to keep him truly warm.

Drayne's body prickled and itched from his throat to his ankles. Now that he was aake the itching was almost enough to distract him from the cold.

But there were no dogs.

There was no sound in the night but the wind.

Nothing threatened. Nothing was near.

The relief he felt now was as intense as the fear in his dream had been.

He flexed his hands, jolts of bright pain shooting

through his fingers as the raw, abraded flesh was pulled and twisted by the movement.

Drayne set his jaw against the pain and forced himself to clench and then extend his fingers, over and over again, until the thin scabs broke and blood began to seep and ooze, making his palms and the pads of his fingers sticky. After a bit the pain was less and his fingers moved more comfortably.

There was no point in trying to go back to sleep now, and he would need the full use of his hands again to make the climb he intended.

There were, he hoped, one, perhaps even two places between himself and the vigilantes where the horses and the dogs could not follow. The one he had found and climbed just before he found this niche in the rock—too shallow to be considered a cave but deep enough to provide at least a little protection from the wind—and with luck too they might not have discovered his deception in the canyon some miles behind. The vigilantes with their strong, quick horses and their pack of vicious dogs might be well behind by now.

He was sure he had given them at least one setback. Now he could give them another. He had another descent to make. He thought he could manage it in the darkness. But last night he had been so tired. Exhausted. So weary he had been close to tears when he found this hole to crawl into.

Drayne had never in his previous experience, never before in his life, known such complete, utter, physical exhaustion. Never. It was something that was new to him and unwelcome. But now, with the few hours of rest, he felt able to go on.

He was hungry. It occurred to him that he would need to find food soon. Water too, of course. Yesterday afternoon he had been able to stop at that creek long enough to fill his empty belly with cold, reviving water. But that was hours gone, and he had no means to carry water.

At the bottom of this next descent he needed to find another rill where he could drink. He needed to find water and food as quickly as possible to recover his exhaustion.

He might be able to trap or catch a fish if he were lucky enough to find another creek. It was a thought. Although he was not sure how a person might go about catching a fish in a stream when he had neither hook nor line.

Drayne had fished as a boy. That had been for sport, not for food. Still, he knew at least a little about it. And he had incentive enough to succeed. The hollow gnawing of hunger in his stomach was more than enough incentive.

If he had time enough, if he was far enough ahead of the men and the dogs, it was at least possible that he might be able to devise some means to capture a fish.

Drayne threw his head back and laughed aloud. He hadn't even a stream to fish in, much less any equipment to fish with. Here he was worrying about how to go about catching something that might as well be a will-o'-the-wisp for all the good his fretting was doing him now.

Still . . . dammit . . . plan. Think. And move.

Yes, that was the thing. Wherever the vigilantes were, they were still somewhere behind. There was still hope that he could escape them. He had to plan for that *and* for feeding himself while he did so.

There was no harm in that. But he could think and plan while he walked.

Drayne crawled out of the niche of hard, cold rock and came upright as joint and bone and muscle protested. The movement gave him an illusory but nonetheless welcome sense of warmth, and he flexed his sore hands again.

He began to think about fish and how a man might go about catching one.

Chapter 11

"Hey!"

Whelan was out of his bedroll and onto his feet in one swift motion, fists balled and a scowl on his face.

"Oops. Sorry, Tom. Didn' see you there." Dennis Forman gave Whelan a silly grin and turned his back, directing the splattering stream of urine the other way. The man was still half drunk from last night's partying and had to lean against an aspen trunk to steady his swaying. He finished, fumbled at his buttons for a moment, and then wobbled back toward the line shack with a flag of blue shirttail protruding from his only partially fastened fly.

Whelan's anger subsided and was replaced with disgust. It wasn't quite dawn yet but there was enough pale light in the sky to be able to make out shapes if not colors. Forman could have been more careful.

Whelan scrubbed the back of his hand over his cheek. Nothing had splashed onto him, exactly, but he felt dirty and uncomfortable nevertheless, and there were some dark speckles of moisture on the edge of his sougan, damn it.

Drunks! Whelan thought with continued disgust. Bunch of damn drunks, most of them. He was regretting all over again that he had agreed to come along, although it was too late to reconsider now. If he pulled away from the posse at this stage, the others would think him a bunch quitter. His pride would not allow that.

But damn them anyhow.

He left his sougan unrolled to dry in the chill air of early morning, walked down to the spring box to wash thoroughly, and then walked well away from the line cabin to do his own morning business.

By the time he returned there was a curl of white smoke lifting from the stovepipe chimney that stuck out of the roof of the dugout. Breakfast would not be long in coming, courtesy of Dor Winston, John Archer, and the supplies they'd had laid in at the dugout. Just the thought of a hot meal warmed Whelan's stomach, and he felt a little better able to face the day to come.

"Good morning, Whelan."

"Mornin', Colonel." McKenzie was on his way into the woods on the same sort of journey Whelan had just made.

"We shall capture the murderer today, eh, Whelan?" McKenzie observed.

Whelan shrugged. "Not if they're still drunk, Colonel."

McKenzie gave Whelan a tight smile. "I noticed your, uh, disapproval last night, Whelan."

"An' I got to say that I *didn't* notice such from you last night, Colonel."

"Of course not, man. Of course not. Encouraged it if the truth be known. And with good reason, I may add."

"I was wondering about that."

McKenzie smiled again. "One blowout and then it's gone, man. The quicker rid of the whiskey the better, I say. Look around you, man. How many of them thought to save a dram or two for tonight, eh?"

"I hadn't thought o' that."

"But I did, Whelan. I did," McKenzie said smugly.

Whelan gave McKenzie the murmur of approval the spare old man so obviously wanted, then touched the brim of his hat and continued down to the line-shack door.

Most of the posse had crammed themselves inside the tiny dugout for the night, preferring the discomfort of the crowding to having to sleep without a roof overhead.

Whelan opened the door and had to step over sleeping men and empty bedrolls to get inside. The place looked and smelled like a boar's nest, and the woodbox by the stove held more empty bottles and shards of broken glass than stove lengths.

There was practically no floor space available for all the bodies and bedding, and the place had a heavy, fetid odor of raw liquor, sour vomit, and flatulence. Whelan wrinkled his nose and stepped carefully across to the stove where Hy Rice was cooking refried beans and stewed tomatoes for breakfast. Beans and rice, mouse-proofed by storing them in old lard tins, were the main staple at the line camps, along with a few items of canned goods. The cans tended to burst during the long, cold winters, though, so only the less desirable things were left behind when the line crews pulled out in the fall. Whelan understood but found himself wishing that Winston and Archer kept a better pantry for their men.

"Help yourself, Tom," Hy offered.

Whelan took a tin plate off a shelf and piled on some of the mashed, brown beans.

"The love apples is hot too," Hy suggested.

"I'll pass on those. Can't ask a gut to take but so much, you know."

Someone on the floor behind him laughed and made a coarse suggestion about the alleged benefits of love apples.

"Us young bucks don't need th' help," another voice put in.

"You will," the first voice said complacently. "Just give it a few years."

"Speak for yourself, Bert. Snow on the roof don't mean there's no fire in the furnace," a third man said.

The rest of them were waking up now to the movement and the noises. Men sat up, yawning and rubbing at their eyes, a few of them hunting around in their bedding in search of bottles that might still hold enough to provide an eye-opener, others groaning onto their feet and stumbling for the door.

Whelan snagged a fork from a box near the stove and carried his plate into the fresher, cleaner air outside.

The warm thoughts he had been having about the prospect of a hot breakfast paled when he looked at the mushy, bland beans. Still, something was better than nothing.

Whelan found a seat on an unsplit chunk of pine by the woodpile and tried a forkful of the stuff.

He found himself looking down-canyon toward the spot where the murderer had disappeared last night and found himself wondering about the man they were pursuing.

The city man would have been almighty grateful for this plate of pap, he suspected.

Whelan found himself wondering where the man was now and how he was faring. It had been the best part of a day and a half now and there had been no time to hunt or trap.

Surely they would get him today. One hungry man afoot in these mountains was no match for a mounted posse with dogs and knowledge of the lay of things.

So today they would surely put the net on him and drag him in.

Behind him a rumble of laughter reached out through the line-shack door. The laughing was followed quickly by an anguished curse from the butt of the joke. Whelan shook his head and took another mouthful of the beans. With this bunch, he conceded, maybe the colonel was right to have encouraged them to drink off the liquor right away.

Not that that should really matter, though. Not if they caught up with the murderer today. If they got him today, they could have their party at the stage stop tonight and old Harry's widow could get a little richer from it.

Whelan finished his breakfast, set the empty plate aside, and began to roll himself that marvelous-tasting first smoke of the day.

Chapter 12

"He's gone and done it again," Kirkland complained. "The sonufabitch has gone and done it again."

The posse was pulled up in a loose bunch of horses and men at the base of a rock wall—not a cliff really, just enough of a wall to stop the horses—with the dogs pawing and yapping at an eighteen-foot-high slab of granite that the killer had somehow climbed.

"That's the third damned time today," Corailis said with disgust. Bert had a fluky sort of temper. He might go weeks at a time with a smile on his face, and it seemed like nothing could ever bother him. On the next breath, though, he might turn and snap a fellow's head off for nothing at all. Now he swiveled sideways in his saddle and gave old Colonel McKenzie a glare like this bother of cliffs and killers was somehow all McKenzie's fault.

More than a few of the boys looked put out by this new need to detour. Whelan suspected that hangovers could have something to do with the humor of the day.

Bill Feeney called his dogs down off the bottom of the little wall. That was getting easier to do than it had been. The pack had accepted the idea that this time their quarry was finding routes they could not follow and that they would be put back onto the scent later.

"Colonel, sir."

"What is it, Feeney?"

"I think I could get my dogs on top right over there. If I climbed up onta that rock there, sir, I think I could give 'em a boost, one by one like, an' they could get up top that way."

"And what good do you think that would do,

Feeney? Do you see a place you could boost the horses onto the top also? Or do you propose to follow the murderer afoot?'' There was a note of sarcasm in McKenzie's voice now. Apparently the onetime militia commander was feeling the frustration of the delays too.

Whelan eased his roan through the crowd until he was close to the colonel's old gelding.

''I have a suggestion, Colonel,'' he said in a soft voice.

McKenzie's answer was a grunt. But he did turn to listen.

''I think this fella is gaining ground on us, Colonel. Losing us every mile or two like this an' making us travel five, six miles to his one 'cause of the dogs.'' Whelan paused and pulled out his makings.

''Go on.''

''Well, what I was thinking, sir, is that I've been paying attention to the way the man's moving. He's running string-straight to the west. Got some idea in mind, I'd say. Some plan or other to get away. Now I don't know what that'd be, but if he keeps pulling ahead of us he just might could manage it.'' He sealed the cigarette with a lick, stuck the thing between his lips, and struck a match. ''What I was thinking, Colonel, is that we should quit playing it his way and see can we get ahead of him. Leapfrog around these delay points of his, see, and get in front of him.''

''You really think you can do that, Whelan?''

Whelan shrugged. ''It's a possibility. Tracking, you know, it isn't so much a matter of trailing along behind something an' trying to catch up with it. Better if you figure out where it's goin' and let it come t' you.'' He carefully extinguished his match before he dropped it to the hard ground under the roan's feet. ''It,'' he said, ''or him. Either one.''

''You sound like you have hunted men before, Whelan.'' McKenzie sounded almost accusing.

Whelan nodded. ''Time to time,'' he conceded.

''Where?'' McKenzie demanded. ''Under what authority?''

Whelan gave the old man a level stare. "Does that matter, Colonel?" He held the stare until McKenzie gave in and looked away.

"No," McKenzie said. "I suppose it does not."

"It was just a thought," Whelan said. He picked up his reins as if to turn the roan away.

"Wait."

Whelan stopped and waited for the old man to go on, drawing on his cigarette and looking toward the top of the rock wall where Harry's killer disappeared.

"There is risk in your idea. The murderer could change direction. We might never pick up his trail again."

"No need to lose it to begin with," Whelan explained. "There's more'n enough of us in this posse. We're only after the one man, and he can't be heavy armed if he's armed at all. I could take a few boys an' slide on ahead to where I think he'll be. You an' the rest of the, uh, command could stay with the dogs and keep on like we been doing. That gives us two chances at him instead o' just the one."

"Division of forces, Mr. Whelan, is seldom a sound decision, tactically or strategically."

"Yeah, well, it was just a thought." Again Whelan took the roan's head to move back toward the rear of the posse.

"Mr. Whelan."

"Yes, Colonel?"

"You may take four men and proceed independently of the main body."

"All right, Colonel."

"Four volunteers, that is."

"Right, Colonel."

Volunteers? What the hell did the old man think they *all* were?

Come to think of it, McKenzie probably did think they were on some sort of sacred mission—for Truth and Justice or some such—with himself their divinely inspired leader. What with his sword and his stiff neck he was acting like he believed that anyhow.

As for Whelan, he couldn't help thinking some about

the poor, scared sonofabitch who was running in front of the dogs too.

An old memory flashed through his thoughts, and he forced it aside, concentrating instead on the question of who he should ask to go with him. Not that it should matter all that much, really. If things worked out right, anybody could do it. If he guessed wrong, nobody could.

What it came down to, then, was whose company he would prefer for the next day or so. He looked toward the sun. Several days to be realistic about it, maybe, because of all the backtracking and side trips they'd had to make chasing behind the damn dogs.

He looked across the bunch toward Lou Kirkland and motioned for Lou to join him, then cast around to see who else out of this crowd he wouldn't mind traveling with.

Chapter 13

Drayne stopped, panting, on the edge of a sheer precipice and looked over the side.

This place was steep enough to stop dogs or horses. Or him. Looking down the heart-stopping drop was like looking down at death.

Particularly considering how extraordinarily tired he was.

His head felt light and swimming, his thoughts slightly detached from the body that struggled to carry out the mind's orders.

That was a result of the hunger, he concluded. He had never been seriously hungry in his life until now, but surely this odd and not really unpleasant sensation came from a lack of food.

The oddest thing about it, he reflected, was that he no longer *felt* especially hungry. Not in his stomach, anyway. Yesterday he had been ravenous, constantly aware of the emptiness and ache in his belly from a lack of food. Today the physical desire for food was nearly absent. Today his interest in food came more from his awareness of the need for sustenance than it did from any physical demand.

It was like his body had already accepted a lack of food to fuel itself as inevitable and was drawing back from the demands it had imposed on him earlier. Yet there was that strange, very slight sense of detachment he felt, as if his body and mind were only tenuously connected.

Damn it, *he needed something to eat.* And soon.

His only hope to escape from the dogs meant climbing and descending places where they could not follow, and for that he needed bodily strength. He needed food.

He looked back over his shoulder, straining his senses for any hint that the dogs were again close.

He hadn't heard the pack or seen the men all morning long. That did not mean they were not on his trail. It only meant that so far he had been able to delay them.

It was not enough to run. He must also survive. In order to run he had to find the food he needed for survival. If he expected to survive, he needed to stop and eat.

Twice this morning he had splashed through creeks where fish no doubt waited to be caught and eaten. Fish that would have provided him with nourishment and a renewal of hope and strength alike. It had occurred to him that he might be able to break a small sapling and use his penknife to fashion a spear point on it, and he had gone so far as to work out the design of the spear tip while he ran. Not a single point or even a single barb whittled into the tip of the sapling. Better to split the tip and fashion a pair of prongs, wedge them apart with a twig perhaps, and barb the inner face of each prong.

With a spear like that he would surely be able to catch a fish. He could gut the thing with the penknife and cook it. He still had matches. Since that first afternoon he had not felt secure enough in his hiding places to build a fire, had not wanted to remain long enough in one place to make proper use of a fire.

And that was the problem with his idea for a pronged fishing spear as well. In order to use it, he would be forced to remain in one location much too long.

He had to run in order to escape. He had to stop in order to survive.

Perhaps worst of all, Drayne was now not entirely confident about his own thought processes.

If the hunger made his thoughts seem detached from his own body, how he could be sure that the hunger-imposed weakness was not also affecting the quality of those thoughts.

He had to suspect himself as well as fear the vigilantes.

He sat, rubber kneed and gasping, and tried to think while he caught his breath again.

"Damn you," he whispered toward the east. " Damn you to hellfire."

After a moment he stood and again looked over the side of the cliff. Even if he had been in his peak of physical condition he would not have attempted this one.

A thought came to him, and he began to smile a bit.

He could not hope to safely get down this face. But he might be able to use it to advantage anyway.

The dogs tracked on the basis of scent, did they not? Of course they did. Wherever he placed a foot, he left a hint of odor behind. So why not leave odor where he had placed no foot.

He let himself down over the edge and stood on the root network of a gnarled, wind-twisted evergreen that was growing out of a crack in the bare rock there and began to strip his clothing off. The pine needles he had been wearing inside his clothing for insulation should be full of the scent of Bryan Drayne by now.

If he could not descend this face, they could.

Quickly he pulled off his clothes, gathered the dry and broken needles by the handful, and spilled them down the cliff below him.

The dogs might, just *might* be fooled into thinking he had somehow made a descent here.

If he did no more than to create a doubt about that, surely the men and horses would have to investigate for his trail at the bottom of this cliff. If that happened, it would be every bit as good a diversion as if he had actually been able to climb down the cliff here.

If it did not work, there was no harm done. The needles were breaking and compacting from use anyway. They no longer warmed him as well as they had when they were fresh. And they could be replaced with no more trouble than it took to pick up fresh ones off the ground and stuff them inside his clothes.

Being without them until evening would even allow him to walk more comfortably through the warmth of the day.

Drayne smiled thinly to himself as he finished disposing of the man-scented pine needles down the side of the cliff, then dressed again and crawled across the uppermost part of the cliff for fifty feet or so before he returned to the level rim above. That was a very small deception but it might help keep the pack from immediately discovering his true scent trail. It was worth trying.

He climbed back on top, winded and shaky again from just that small amount of exertion, and turned north along the rim, walking with much more determination than energy now.

His legs were weak and his breathing labored, but he was able to go on. Hungry, crazy, or whatever, damn it, he *would* go on. Whatever it took, he would go on until he was free or until he was dead.

He swore to himself that he would.

Chapter 14

It was late afternoon and Drayne had been resting in the last of the dying sunshine for a good ten minutes now.

The need to keep moving, to escape, kept running through his thoughts, but it was difficult to convince himself to actually do anything about it. Sitting felt so very, very good. And it had been so very long since he had actually heard the mournful baying of the pack of dogs.

His eyes sagged shut for a moment, and he felt the tension in his shoulders subside. His muscles relaxed, and he began to slump forward.

He came wide-awake with an abrupt start of fear.

Not of the dogs this time but of himself. Of his own weakness.

It would be bad enough if the vigilantes caught him. It would be infinitely worse if he were to defeat himself.

He came onto his feet, heart pounding in sudden worry, and turned to look back the way he had come. As before, as it had been all day, there was nothing back there to see. Nothing but rock, tree, and near-cloudless sky. He shivered, the chill having nothing to do with temperature, and took one step foward, then another.

"Move," he whispered out loud to himself. "Freedom is movement. Freedom is over there in Idaho."

He felt slightly silly to discover that he was talking to himself. Not just thinking these things but actually vocalizing them. For as long as he could remember he had heard the jokes about people who talked to themselves. Now he was doing it.

Daft as it might be, though, there was also something comforting about it.

"And what's the harm if I damn well feel like it, anyhow?" he asked himself, striving to maintain a normal speaking tone in this one-sided conversation.

He knew good and well that the only people likely to be out here in these awful mountains were the vigilantes, and they seemed to be many miles behind. No one could possibly overhear. Yet he had to stifle an impulse to whisper.

As it was, the closest he could come to a normal voice was a muted speech, louder than a whisper but considerably softer than a true conversational tone. More like the quiet tone one would use in a theater lobby while an orchestra played beyond the doors.

That realization annoyed him. He squared his shoulders and raised his chin, even his westward-moving stride strengthening for the moment, and loudly declared, "No harm done. Damn it. No harm done." And then, his voice rising into a shout, "No harm done!"

The sound of the shouted words disappeared into the barren wilderness around him, the brief touch of its humanity swallowed up and lost forever, not even echoing back to him, no ears but his own to capture and hold this record of his presence here.

He shuddered, and his eyes dropped toward the ground in front of his moving feet as he walked stubbornly on toward the west.

He felt immeasurably alone, and it occurred to him that perhaps he had at last discovered the answer to the timeless question about the tree falling in the forest. When there were no ears to hear, it didn't *matter* if there was sound or if there was not. Drayne laughed, a short, sharp bitter bark of additional sound, and continued to walk, trying to plan as he did so.

The sun was low now. The heat of it would be quickly lost. He would have to replace the pine needles in his clothes for warmth. Soon he would have to find a place to sleep.

He was tired. So horribly tired. He needed to sleep at least a part of the night. He wanted to find a cave, an overhang, some nest of rock into which he could crawl and rest and then resume when he woke.

He looked toward the sky and then toward the country ahead of him. There would be something. Any form of shelter would do.

Now if only he could find something to eat. Surely there had to be something in this country that was edible from the wild. If only he knew what it might be.

Moving now with short, jerky steps, shoulders slumped and head down, Drayne forged slowly forward, one pace at a time.

Chapter 15

"What're you doing now, Tom?"

Whelan took his time about answering. He was sitting on the roan with his knee hooked over the saddle horn and his reins slack, a cigarette dangling from the corner of his mouth.

"Shouldn't we be . . . I don't know . . . chasing the sonufabitch?"

"I'm looking," Whelan said softly. He sounded disconnected, as if he had been only half paying attention to them.

"Shouldn't we be doing something?" Roger Burris persisted.

Whelan was already regretting that he had agreed to bring Burris along. It had been Kirkland's idea, and Whelan had made no objection at the time. He suspected the reason Lou wanted Burris with them was so he could talk to Burris about buying some surplus hay before the hard cold hit and the prices went up. Lou probably wanted to buy the hay on tick, to be paid when his calves were sold. Whelan did not know Burris all that well himself. He was beginning to think he didn't want to.

"What'd you have in mind, Roger?"

"I don't know. Something. Isn't that the idea? Isn't that why we're here? To chase the murderer?"

"Uh-huh," Whelan said patiently. "That's why we're here."

"Well?"

Whelan sighed and flicked the ash off his smoke. "If you see him, Roger, you go right at him."

"But . . ."

"What I'm doing right now, Roger, is looking at the lay o' things. Trying to figure out where the guy'll go next."

"Isn't that what the dogs was for?"

"Nope," Whelan explained. "The dogs figure where the man has *been.* What I'm trying to do now is guess where he's *gonna* be."

"Now how the hell do you figure to do that?"

"We know a bit about him. We know he's headed west. Been moving west ever since he run out of the stage stop with Harry dead behind him and half the county chasing after him. The man's been going west. And we know he's a climber. He knows Feeney and those dogs are behind him, and I bet he knows we're glued to our saddles too. So he's been climbing up an' down cliffs to throw us every chance he's got. So what I'm trying to work out now, Roger, is where to set and wait for him."

"One place should be about as good as the next, shouldn't it?"

"Now you see, that's the thing. It isn't. Like across this flat here. Man on the run, traveling afoot and knowing there's dogs and horses chasing, he isn't gonna want to expose himself across a wide ol' flat like this. He's gonna keep to the tight places. Places that he can maybe lose us in a hurry if he has to. Like along rim tops and ledges and gully bottoms where he might scramble away and we couldn't follow. So that's what we're looking for now. Places like that that'd take him west from where he was last."

Burris grunted something that could have been either agreement or complaint.

Behind Burris, Luke Rice leaned over to say something to his brother and got a nod back from Hy.

"We know a place that might fit what you're looking for, Tom."

Whelan raised an eyebrow.

" 'Bout a mile, mile and a half north of here. Just the other side of that mountain. There's a bunch of finger canyons branch out on the northwest side of that knob. We worked awhile for Jess Arleiter and used to use a line shack he kept over there. Called it the Turkeyfoot because of the way those finger ridges run."

Whelan kicked his knee off the horn and reset his foot in the stirrup. Then he stood to take a better look off to the east, the direction he expected the killer to be coming from.

The man would definitely want to avoid this open flat. It would be logical for him to follow the base of the mountain knob that lay ahead of where the possemen now sat. If that knob fed into the finger ridges so that a man on foot could see . . .

"Let's go take a look."

They had to call for Kirkland to join them. Lou had left his horse with Hy and gone off behind a tree to do his business.

"I'm coming. Keep your drawers on."

"Better you should get yours on."

Whelan grinned as Kirkland came waddling out from behind a juniper still in the process of pulling his jeans up and trying to get them buttoned and his suspenders strapped back in place.

All in all Kirkland was a pretty good old boy. He was always broke, was likely the sort who would stay that way even if beef went to half a dollar a pound, but that never stopped him from being generous. When times got tight a man could hit Lou up for work and never get a turndown even if Lou had no need for the labor or cash money to pay the hire. Whatever he had he was willing to share. In fact he'd been the first man to offer Tom Whelan a bed and a job when Whelan first came into this country, and Tom had liked him ever since.

Kirkland retrieved his reins from Hy and tossed them over his horse's neck. He winked at Tom and stuck his hands deep into his pockets. Whelan started to chuckle even before Lou performed his favorite parlor trick. Parlor trick, that is, if a fella didn't mind having a horse in his parlor.

Lou feigned a look of slightly impish innocence and sauntered over to his pony. Without taking his hands out of his pockets or even seeming to change his stride, he stepped into the stirrup, swung onto the saddle with a lanky, easy flow of motion, and then commenced to grin.

"How the hell . . . ?" Roger Burris blurted.

Whelan and the Rice boys began to laugh. They had seen Kirkland do that time and time again, but the first time you saw it you always had to think it was impossible. It *looked* impossible but naturally wasn't. Lou did it easily every time. And if the truth be known, Whelan could manage it sometimes. Although he always did his practicing very much in private and had never let on to anyone that he had ever so much as tried it.

Kirkland grinned again, took his hands out of his pockets, and picked up the reins from the neck of his horse. "Well? I'm waitin' on you boys."

Whelan led them north toward the knob where the Rice boys said they would find those finger rims and maybe Harry's killer as well.

Chapter 16

"I got a question," Burris said. He leaned forward to dip into the heavy, honey-colored oil left in the can of sardines they shared for lunch. He dipped half a cracker into the thick oil, popped the dripping cracker into his mouth and sucked the fishy-tasting grease off the ball of his thumb.

"What's that, Roger?" Kirkland asked. Kirkland was sitting next to Burris. The Rice brothers were side by side and Whelan completed the loose circle. Hy was busy wrapping up what was left of a chunk of rat cheese he had contributed to the meal. At Whelan's insistence they had eaten a cold meal and built no fire to gather around. Even so, by habit they had ranged themselves around the spot where a fire would have been had they built one.

"What happens when we catch the sonofabitch?" Burris asked.

There was no immediate answer from the others. The Rice boys seemed no more comfortable with Burris than Whelan was, and Kirkland was waiting for Tom to respond. Whelan was busy rolling a cigarette.

"You don't want to talk about it? All right. But I think I got a right to know," Burris went on. "I mean, it's something we haven't actually said. Not right out. But I think we should. Do we hang the man ourselves or wait for the rest of the posse to join up? It's a matter of . . . responsibility. You know?"

"Nobody's gonna hang," Whelan said softly. He twisted the tips of his cigarette, licked it, and struck a match.

"Just what are we s'posed to do then?" Burris persisted. "All the rest of the boys was talking about hanging. So what are we s'posed to do? Find the guy and give him a stern talking to? Tell him it isn't nice to go around murdering folks' neighbors?"

Whelan looked across the fireless circle toward Burris, wishing for the moment that Lou had not wanted this one along. Not that there was much point in thinking about that now.

"We come out here to catch the man, not punish him," Whelan said. "Vigilance justice went outta style a long time ago."

Burris said nothing, but he was frowning like he disagreed. He examined the greasy shine on the ball of his thumb, then wiped the lingering oil on his trousers.

"You got something to say about that, Burris?" Whelan demanded. His tone of voice was not friendly. Lou Kirkland searched the ground beside him for a leaf or twig to fiddle with.

"I just thought . . ."

"You ever seen a vigilance committee at work, Burris?"

The man shook his head. He had been in the country . . . this was his second winter coming . . . call it a year and a half. It was known that he came out from Illinois. Likely another farmer or small-town merchant who'd gotten his head full of dreams borrowed straight out of *Harper's* or the Buntline stories or even, God forbid, *Uncle Billy's.* He'd showed up with a couple dozen heavy mares and a mostly decent Percheron stud and said he figured to breed draft stock. He never flashed a roll exactly, but he seemed to have some money behind him while he was beginning the breeding program. It took a long time to get a line of stock established.

But that was about all Whelan knew about Burris.

Come to think of it, he realized, it was considerably more than he knew about most of his neighbors. Few talked all that much about their pasts. It was a habit of the country. And one Tom Whelan appreciated.

Of course a man could always guess some things that weren't said. The Rice boys now, they had come over from southern Idaho, northern Nevada, southeast

Oregon, some part of that country. You could see that easy in their buckaroo gear. They wore short chink chaps, for instance, with long fringes and fancy inlays of different color leather, and most of their small riding gear was hand braided out of horsehair.

It would've been cheating to make such guesses about Kirkland. Lou talked about himself now and then. He'd come up from Kansas, but a long time back. Delivered some beeves to Deadwood while the Black Hills run was still active and stayed with the thought to making a fortune. Drifted over through Wyoming and on up into Montana, moving along a bit at a time, first as the Indian tribes were resettled and moved out, then being pushed from behind as the dryland farmers took over. Lou still hoped to make his fortune, but he was quite a ways from it. Likely he would have been closer to that goal by now if he wasn't so free-handed.

But Lou and the Rices, they were all from country Whelan understood, the Rices with their centerfire saddles and Lou with his parlor-chair heavy double rig and a tie-fast style borrowed from the old-time Texans he learned the business from.

It was Burris whose past baffled Whelan. Burris whose ways were not eastern exactly, but just a little bit different.

Whelan pulled on his cigarette and dropped his chin a bit so the brim of his hat would keep the others from staring at him while he thought. He really shouldn't have come along with this posse. There was work enough at home that he could've been doing instead. He hadn't really wanted to come to begin with, and now here he was halfway leading a piece of the chase.

That damn sure hadn't been any part of what he intended.

Not that there would be any pulling out of it now, though. If he did that . . . he might as well just keep on going if he rode away from the posse now. Take it right on out of the country, because he would be thought of as a quitter if he left now.

In a country where a man needed the goodwill of his neighbors just to get along from one season to the next, he might just as well up and leave as to let himself be thought a quitter.

Now that he'd started it he had to carry it on through. But there sure were things he would rather be doing.

"All right," Burris was saying. "You asked me have I seen a vigilance committee, and I haven't. Which is no fault of mine. But what I heard about them wasn't all bad. I expect I don't know what you're getting at, Whelan."

Whelan tipped his head back and looked at the man for a moment. "What you heard about them wasn't all bad, Burris? What you heard about them was all shit, then." He went back to paying attention to his cigarette.

"You want to explain that, mister? Or just leave it laying there like a dead snake in the middle of the parlor floor?"

Whelan sighed. The man honestly didn't know. It wasn't his fault that he didn't know. He hadn't been here during those times.

"There's some others in the main body of the posse older than me that could tell you some things, Burris. How the committees started all pure and good and ended up poison."

"But you're the one that has the opinion that counts here and now, Whelan," Burris frowned. "I'm not trying to get smart-ass with you, Tom. I'm trying to understand what we're doing here."

Whelan thought about that for a moment. And nodded. The man wasn't trying to come on hard. He just didn't know.

"All right," Whelan said. "One for-instance, then. One that I happen to know about."

Burris leaned forward attentively. For that matter, the Rice boys were looking interested too. Whelan couldn't see Kirkland's face. Lou was staring down toward his lap where he was braiding some pine needles together, pretending not to be paying attention.

"When I was just little it was near the end of the committees' influence. I guess you've read some about those times, but not much of what was written was true.

The committees had gone out of hand. They started out to make the country cleaner for the decent folks to live in. Then they got powerful, and if a member had a beef with his neighbor, he'd just lay an accusation, and the committee would ride off and punish the neighbor. There wasn't no trials. No charges laid nor answers given. The committees would just hear the charge an' go levy the punishment, right there on the spot. A lot o' men hanged or burned. Some women and kids too, for that matter. Fire don't care who it gets.

"Anyhow, this one time that I'm thinking of, an' I won't drag up names or places as it wouldn't serve no purpose, but this one time there was a man, used to be chairman of his local committee, he got word that this neighbor, who was new to the country and now a part of the committee, was fixing to run the man's best bull into his own herd to service the neighbor's cows. And this man figured to teach the neighbor a lesson. That's all he wanted to do, you understand. Just give the man a warning. No hangings nor ropings nor anything like that. Just a lesson." Whelan wished he had some of Lou's rye whiskey, but he didn't.

"So the committee got together this one night and pulled their hoods on, and since it was just a warning and a lotta fun, they even put hoods on some o' their sons and let them ride along on the fun. Kinda break the boys in to the way things were, you see."

Burris and the Rice brothers nodded. Kirkland was looking up now too.

"What they figured to do, you see, was post a note of warning and fire the man's haystack so to make sure he'd get the message strong.

"Well, they done 'er. Broke out the liquor bottles and laughed and talked the whole way to this other place. Had a helluva good time, they did. An' when they got there, a couple of men fired shots in the air to make sure nobody came outta the house and a couple others got down an' fired the hay, and everybody was having a good time.

"Except the wind went an' shifted and some sparks flew over and set off the roof of the house these new people had built, and it went to burning. And the folks inside must've been so scared that they wouldn't run out or else the place burned too quick for them or something, because the next thing you know the whole outfit was on fire, and the roof fell in on them people, and there was a whole family burned up. Or near about a whole family. There was one kid left alive, and he had burns all down his legs and like to died except for a doctor in Great Falls. And I expect he's scarred over it to this day, deeper than any marks on the surface go through. Scarred to the bone is what I'd guess."

Whelan shut up, feeling a little embarrassed now that he had talked so much and said that about the scarring going deeper than what a man could see.

The others looked away, not wanting to meet his eyes now, except for Lou, who said, "But dammit, Tom, I've washed off in more than one creek beside you. You don't have no scars on your legs. Or noplace else that I've seen."

Whelan looked at him blankly for a moment until it dawned on him what the others must be thinking. He shook his head.

"I wasn't in that house, Lou. I wasn't the kid that survived the fire."

"But we thought . . . least I thought . . ."

"I was one of the kids that was carried along that night, Lou. I was one that my daddy told me to hop down an' light the haystack."

"Jesus," Burris muttered. He wriggled his shoulders like he had just gotten a chill.

"Was the man guilty?" Luke asked. "The man the committee was wanting to warn?"

"Yes," Whelan admitted. "He was guilty of trying to take the use of some bull semen. Seems a helluva price to pay for that, though."

Kirkland looked at Whelan. "We aren't a vigilance committee, Tom. You want to remember that. And it's no innocent family we're out here chasing. We're after a man that murdered a neighbor of ours. He's got no woman or kids with him. It's just us against a killer. Don't try and make more of it than it is."

"I don't want to," Tom said. "I just don't want—"

"Damn!" Hy Rice blurted, interrupting. "Lookee there." Hy was grinning and pointing and trying to reach for his rifle, all at the same time.

"It's him," Luke whispered loudly as he too reached for his Winchester.

Several hundred yards away the killer had come out into the open. Just about where they expected him to.

He was too far away to get a good look at him, but this was not country where anyone else was going to be afoot and coatless and moving along at that slow, tired pace.

He wore dark trousers and a white shirt and no hat, and he was carrying no weapons that Whelan could see.

The killer was moving with the slow, dogged, head-down trudge of near exhaustion. He had come out of the rocks at the base of the knob, probably had been walking among them or they would have seen him sooner, and now was heading out onto the ridges where Tom Whelan and his bunch of the posse were waiting.

All they had to do now was let him come to them. They could wrap him up and carry him back to join the rest of the posse, and from there on it would be up to the sheriff and the lawyers.

Whelan smiled. It was over with, and he was glad.

He went to say something to that effect.

But his eyes widened and his jaw dropped open, and too late he made a lunge for Roger Burris's back.

Burris had his Winchester to his shoulder and the hammer earred back and was already lining up to put a bullet in the killer's chest.

Whelan dived for the gun, intending to wrestle it away from Burris so they could just sit where they were and let the man practically walk into their camp to be taken, but the slab-sided saddle carbine bellowed and bucked against Burris's shoulder before Whelan could reach him, and far down the ridge Harry's killer flopped over backward, twisting and falling to the ground.

Now that the man was out of sight, already grassed by Burris's bullet, Luke and Hy began to bash away with their own Winchesters, making noise and smoke but not accomplishing much else, firing like they'd suddenly gone to war or something.

"Quit," Whelan yelled. "Jesus Christ, will you people quit it!"

The Rice boys quit firing, and Lou Kirkland never had shot although he had his rifle in his hands now. Roger Burris gave Whelan a dirty look for having tried to jump him like that and just to prove that he didn't have to take orders from Whelan snapped one more shot in the general direction of the fallen killer.

Then they all came to their feet and brushed off their britches and gave each other smiles of grim satisfaction before they set off toward where the killer had gone down.

All of them, that is, except Whelan, who felt about half sick, and Kirkland, who paused long enough to give Tom a shrug of apology before he hurried to catch up with the others.

Whelan left his Marlin in the scabbard—there were guns enough in hand already—and walked after the rest of them.

Of them all he was probably the only one who hoped they would find Harry's killer still alive.

Chapter 17

Drayne gasped and rolled onto his side, his hand automatically feeling for the place of stinging warmth on his chest.

He hurt like hell, and already he could feel blood flowing.

So this was what it was like to be shot.

It was not at all what he would have expected.

Old men who had been in the old war . . . and younger men who had been to Cuba or all the way across the globe to the Philippines . . . they all said how when a man was shot he only felt the impact and that it wasn't until later that the hurting began.

Well, no matter what they said, he could feel this and feel it right damn now.

It hurt, dammit. It stung like fire, and he was bleeding too. His breath came in short, hard gulps, and he was beginning to feel woozy.

Where had the shot come from? Where were they? And where were the dogs? Why hadn't he heard any dogs?

Time to think about that later. He could still move.

He hurt, but he wasn't dead. Not yet, he wasn't. But he would be if they caught him.

He was lying stretched out flat on the ground. So maybe they couldn't see him now, but they would be coming. He knew that. They would be coming. He had only seconds to get away.

There was a slope down into the canyon below. He'd been walking the rim, looking for places steep enough to throw off the dogs but not so steep that he couldn't get down them.

So far he hadn't found what he wanted. But where he was would just have to do. He thought dogs might make it down. He doubted that a horse could. He took half a moment to peer down at the fresh, bright blood that was smeared on his palm from where he had touched his chest. Oddly, there was less of it than he had expected. Less blood and more pain.

Think about that later. Plan later. If there was a later.

He rolled the rest of the way over onto his belly and began to crawl and wiggle across the rocks and gravel of the rim. Toward the sharp slope down into the canyon. They were much too close and he was much too weak to think about trying to outrun them. The slope down off this rim was his only chance. Desperately, panting and gasping, Drayne crawled belly down to the ground in the only direction that held out any hope whatsoever. He grunted with effort as he crawled and tried to steel himself against the sharp jolts of pain that shot through his chest with every movement.

He had to get away from them. He had to.

Chapter 18

He slid the last dozen feet on his backside, hit the bottom, and rolled. The jolting, twisting movement sent fresh pain through his chest and he winced, half convinced that he was already dying. It would have been easier to lie there where he fell and wait for the vigilantes to come finish him off.

Drayne grunted and rolled over, came to his knees pushing up with his arms. It was odd, but both arms seemed to be working just fine, even though he had been shot high in the chest. The bleeding seemed to have stopped already too. Gingerly he opened the buttons of his shirt and took a look at the wound.

Wounds was more like it. The right side of his chest was peppered with a number of small and painful—but obviously not truly dangerous—punctures and abrasions. There was no single, large bullet hole, rather a number of very small ones.

He must have been shot with pellets from a shotgun, he concluded. It hadn't been a rifle or revolver after all.

The small wounds stung. But now that he realized they were not serious, they did not even seem to hurt as much as they had.

He crouched by a clump of some scrub and peered up toward the rim. The slope was steeper than it had looked from up there, although nowhere steep enough to keep a pack of dogs from coming down it. He had come down more by sliding than climbing. And in a hurry. The men who had shot him would be up there looking for him. He had to get under cover so they could not see him from above.

He came to his feet, reeling slightly from the

combination of hunger and shock, and staggered into the middle of the canyon where dense brush should make it impossible for anyone above to see him.

The foliage was different here. Not the junipers, spruces, and pines he had been passing through on the high rims. Here the vegetation was mostly deciduous and of a kind he did not recognize. The leaves were already changing color, but few of them had fallen. There was ample cover to turn aside prying eyes.

Better yet, there was a small spring at the head of the narrow canyon. The flow of water was more than likely responsible for the thick brush here.

Drayne followed the rill far enough into the brush to feel reasonably safe from the eyes above, then dropped to his knees and drank of the cold water.

The refreshment it gave him went far beyond the value of the drink itself. The water provided a measure of hope too. He drank deeply, forcing himself overfull, then took a moment to cup some of the flow into his hand and apply it to the stinging wounds on his chest.

There was very little pain now, and the cool water felt good.

If only he had something to eat now . . .

He had no time to think about that, he knew.

The hunters and their pack were close. Somehow he had failed to hear the pursuit of the dogs, but they could not be far away. Drayne grimaced and pulled himself to his feet.

He had to evade them. He had to plan.

Until now he had climbed or descended to throw them off scent. By now they would be expecting that. Perhaps some recognized habit like that was what allowed them to be lying in wait for him. Because now that he was able to think about it rationally, he realized that the gunshot, and all those that had followed so quickly behind the first, had come from *ahead* of him.

Somehow they had guessed where he might be and were there waiting for him.

Somehow now he had to change his pattern if he expected to get away while they were so terribly, terribly close.

He looked toward the nearer wall of the canyon. The truth was that he doubted he could climb it now even if he wanted to. Even if he *needed* to. He was simply too weak now. His knees barely supported him on more or less level ground. Climbing again was out of the question, at least for the moment.

He looked down at the creek. Running water would wash away a scent, he understood. And if he could somehow lay a false trail, then use the water to hide his scent . . . especially if the men hunting him were anticipating that he would climb out of the canyon . . .

He began to smile.

Of course. And it just might work.

He could not leave the protection of the stream-side brush now. Not with the men above looking for him. But if he could follow the creek downstream for a safe distance . . . and then find a wall that would be suitably difficult to scale . . . and walk to that wall, leaving scent behind, and then walk *back* to the creek . . . why, he might just be able to walk downstream *in* the creek from there and get away from them.

It just might work.

Best of all, it was something that was possible within the limits of his strength.

It was something that he just might be able to manage.

Drayne cupped his hands and drank again, filling his stomach to the point of discomfort, then quickly washed his face and neck and chest again.

Then, very carefully, he began to make his way downstream, walking part of the time in the thin flow of water but making sure that now and again he stepped on the bank where he would leave a scent and perhaps a track for them to find.

That, after all, was part of his plan. But after the false trail was laid, he would have to be careful to leave no trace of himself on the dry bank.

Now if only he could find something to eat . . . He tried to content himself with the idea that this particular creek, at least, was too small to hold fish.

The attempt at self-deception was only partially successful.

He was hungry. Lord God, he was hungry.

He stumbled down the streambed, weak but determined.

They would not catch him. They would *not.*

Chapter 19

"Is he dead?" Whelan asked as he caught up with the others.

Burris looked away, staring down into the canyon below. It was Lou Kirkland who answered. "We don't know, Tom."

"Don't know. What the hell d'you mean, you don't know?" Whelan took a few steps closer and realized for the first time there was no body on the ground where the men were standing.

"I got him, though," Burris said. "You can see the blood for yourself. Right there it is."

He pointed. There was a dark red smear already drying on a slab of gray rock where the killer had gone down. The blood seemed to lead back toward the mountain knob, as if the killer had been dragging himself off in that direction before he somehow stanched the light flow.

"Looks like you didn't any more than pink him," Whelan said. "There sure ain't much blood there."

"I caught him a good one," Burris protested. "I was holding square on his chest."

Whelan shook his head. "At two hundred yards?" He took a closer look at Burris's Winchester. "That a forty-four-forty?"

The man nodded.

"At two hundred yards you'd be lucky to hit him in the boots with a chest hold and one of them old forty-four-forties. You'd be asking a lot of a thirty-thirty at that range, much less one of those old crocks. Hell, man, I can chunk rocks farther'n a forty-four-forty can throw lead."

"I tell you, Whelan, I had a good bead on him, an' I know this rifle. I got him good. Shit, he's prob'ly dead by now. Just lived long enough to crawl off someplace. We'll find him under some brush, like a rabbit that you've shot an' couldn't find afterward. You'll see." As if to demonstrate his point, Burris walked a little ways back toward the mountain and used the barrel of his Winchester to begin lifting the thick, fanlike branches of the low junipers and peering under them.

The Rice boys glanced uneasily toward Whelan, then joined Burris in the search for a dead body. Kirkland gave Tom a silent look and then a shrug. He turned and went to help in the search.

Whelan stayed where he was for a moment.

The blood on the stone at least gave them an exact reference point. And they had all seen him fall. There was no doubting that much.

Whelan stood over the stain and looked back at where they had been waiting. At this distance it was difficult to make out the camp, even knowing what he was looking for. The horses were out of sight. It was no wonder the killer had not spotted them.

Whelan's concentration moved closer to the place where the killer had dropped out of sight. He had seen some dirt and gravel fly when the Rice boys were shooting. He was sure of that, not quite so sure about what had happened when Burris shot, since then he had been intent on trying to stop the man from shooting and not paying attention to the killer.

Fifteen, twenty yards in front of the place where the killer had been walking he could see several places where the ground had been disturbed by rifle shots falling far short of their intended mark. Those could have been Luke and Hy's shots. Or they could as easily have been Roger Burris's. There simply was no way to tell now.

Hell, he thought, Burris could have put a bullet into the man's chest, as he believed he had done. Or he could as easily have clipped him with ricocheting specks of lead and gravel. They probably would not know the truth of that until they caught up with the killer.

Whelan walked over to the edge of the rim and looked

down into the canyon. The man could have crawled or even fallen down there. But there was no sign of him. Not at the bottom or anywhere along the steep slope.

Could the guy have . . . ? Whelan shook his head. Not very damn likely. They knew he had been hit. They had all seen him hit and go down. The question was how bad.

Looking at the slope beneath his boots now, Whelan knew that no horse could make it dewn that one, and for a man to make it, the fellow would have to be mighty agile or he sure wouldn't make it in one piece. Wounded, likely weakened as well by exposure—they had all been able to see plain as day that the killer had no coat or covering except a white shirt—and hunger too probably . . . there was no likelihood that the man would have tried to get down this slope. None at all that he could have made it. If he'd tried to go this way, he should be lying in a heap down there at the bottom this very minute, and Whelan couldn't see a body there or any sign that one had slid down.

And Burris was certainly right about one thing. A man going out hunting could put down a bull elk most as big as a grown steer and with antlers like a damn tree and then spend half a day trying to find the thing in brush no thicker than was growing right here.

And a wounded man, with all the cunning that implied, why, he was apt to run like hell to keep from being caught, if he was able to move like that, or else hole up in a place you wouldn't think big enough to hide a coyote.

Either way, what they needed to be doing right now was trying to find him. The boys were right about that.

Still, when Whelan joined them once again, he couldn't help saying, even though he knew that he shouldn't, "You know, Burris, there was no need to shoot like you done. The man was coming to us. All we had t' do was wait for him to walk into our camp. We coulda took him without a fuss."

"You got all the answers, don't you, Whelan?" Burris said venomously. He half turned away, looking behind a jumble of flat rocks. As he did so he leaned closer to Luke and mumbled something like "smart-ass sonofabitch."

Whelan took a step foward. His intention was to explain. He felt no particular need to apologize exactly but he did want to explain. Burris apparently misunderstood the approach.

The man spun back to face Whelan and threw a haymaker.

Whelan, taken completely by surprise, took the wild, looping punch flush on the side of his face and was knocked off his feet by the force of it. He rolled, scrambled to his feet and drove forward to meet the angry, oncoming Burris. The two men grappled and went down, holding and kicking and trying to pummel one another.

Burris got in another glancing punch to the side of Whelan's head and Tom threw himself on top of Burris's body, burying his forehead in the man's throat and sending short, chopping body blows into Burris's gut. He was still swinging when Kirkland grabbed him by the shoulders and pulled him away while the Rice boys were busy restraining Burris.

The scrap had taken mere seconds but the men were panting from exertion and emotion.

"Quit, dammit. Both of you quit now," Kirkland barked.

Whelan was willing. But only if Burris was, damn the man. Fighting with his fists, for Christ's sake.

Tom Whelan probably had not been in two fistfights in his life, and those times would have been while he was still wearing short pants. In cow country a man was taught that scuffling was for dogs. Men fought with guns or knives or even ropes. But never with their hands. That farmer Burris had gone and *hit* him.

Trembling slightly, he reached up and touched his ear. It was sore, and he could feel blood running along his jawline from a cut. That was maybe the worst of it. Burris was heaving for breath and he looked like he was hurting some, but dammit he had come out the better in the brawl for he wasn't bleeding anywhere.

"Don't you ever try to jump me again, Whelan," Burris hissed.

"Jump you. Jump you? Mister, you'd best understand here and now the way things are in this country. Do I want you that bad I'll call you out, face-to-face, and I'll have a gun in my hand, not back with the horses. D'you understand me?"

"Both of you shut up an' calm down now," Kirkland said. "Roger, you got to understand that things is different here from what you're used to. And Tom, you got to understand that Roger did what he thought was best. That's all. The both of you was only trying to do what you thought was best." Lou forced a smile. "Why, we surely aren't gonna let some murderer come between us. Not that either one of you wants to see Harry's killer get away. No question about that. You're just of different minds about what oughta be done, that's all. An' we all agree that the killer's got to be caught and punished. That's the main thing, right? Now the two of you shake hands and forget this business. It was just a misunderstanding, that's all." Kirkland was still smiling. He took Whelan's sleeve and tugged him a step closer to Burris, then slapped Burris on the shoulder and pushed him forward a bit until the two were face-to-face again.

Whelan set his jaw and stubbornly waited for Burris to extend his hand first. Then Tom reached out and accepted it.

Damn farmer, he was thinking.

They did shake, though.

Whelan coughed and spat. "I shouldn't have mentioned that about taking the guy easy," he said—although as explanation and not apology. "We hadn't talked about it. And I expect you were thinking he might turn away before he got to us, headed down into the canyon or something."

"Yeah. Well, maybe I could've waited a bit to see. I seen him and I shot. We were shooting at him before. It just seemed like the right thing to do. I, uh, I'm sorry I hit you."

Whelan nodded. He paused for a moment, then grinned and rubbed at the side of his jaw where the blood from the cut was no longer flowing but was becoming sticky as it dried. "You got me a pretty good lick there."

"You ain't exactly a weakling," Burris admitted, gingerly touching his stomach and side.

"Hadn't we better get back to looking for the murderer?" Luke put in. "The guy could be getting away while we're here chasing our own tails."

"Yeah. You're right, Luke. Let's find the sonofabitch and go home." Whelan began to kick through the brush, looking not for a man but for a piece of a man, the way you do when you hunt. You look for an eye or an ear or the flick of a tail, in this case a boot or a hand or a scrap of white shirt showing someplace where there should only be dirt or rock or roots.

The killer was wounded. He couldn't have gotten far.

Chapter 20

Drayne crept back to the stream and the protective cover of the brush. He was trembling with fear while he was exposed to view from above. If those vigilantes had followed the rims out this far . . . He could neither see nor hear anything from above, though. He might be safe. Just might be. And he absolutely had to leave that false trail. Once they reached the bottom of the canyon, he had to make them waste time by drawing them back to the top again while they searched for his trail. That was his only hope.

But, Lord, he was afraid. He felt vulnerable, his small wounds stinging again now in his fear, and there was a tiny, circular area on his back, high between his shoulder blades, that felt hot and sore in the imagined anticipation of a bullet striking him there if one of them should be watching, damn them.

He hurried back to the stream as quickly as his weakened legs could take him, bent low to the ground and moving at a hunched, scurrying pace. He did not begin to breathe any easier until he was under the shelter of the leaves and his feet were back in the chill water of the creek.

His shoes were wet, had been for the better part of a mile now, and he was sure he was beginning to get blisters. Not that he could feel very much yet. His feet were numbed by the continued cold of the water.

He stopped, standing ankle deep in the creek, and bent forward at the waist, pausing there while he tried to get his breath and let his heart rate slow.

Then, when he felt up to it again, he continued to walk downstream, being very careful now to leave no footprint or trace of scent on the banks beside the narrow creek. The footing was difficult. His feet were numb and the rocks in the streambed were slick. Once he fell, crying out in protest but remembering even as he slipped that he must at all costs remain in the water. If he so much as threw a hand onto the dry bank to support himself, the deception might be ruined.

He fell with a splash, soaking himself head to toe in the cold water so that he was quickly chilled and shivering. The cold water shocked him, and he bounced back upright almost at once. It would have been a relief to be able to stop and lie down for the briefest of moments. But not in the middle of a flow of icy water.

Drayne shook himself and shivered. He heard a low, mournful sound that frightened him. It took a few moments before he realized that he was making the noises himself. He was whimpering out loud in the silence of the wilderness.

He clamped his jaws shut against the whining sounds of defeat and forced back an impulse toward tears.

"Damn you," he whispered toward the distant rim where he had last seen his pursuers. "Damn you."

Shakily he began to walk again along the slick, stony bottom of the creek bed, moving now to keep warm as well as to leave the hunters behind.

He wanted desperately to stop, to rest, simply to lie down. It would almost be worth dying if only he could lie down to rest in warm, dry comfort for a few minutes. Almost worth it. That was the thing. Almost. And even if he did stop, even if he did lie down to rest, he would be neither warm nor dry. He would be as miserable stopping as he would be moving now.

He plunged on between the narrow banks of the creek, scarcely looking now to either side, head hanging low and all thought driven from him except to keep moving forward, to continue placing one foot ahead of the other.

"Damn you," he moaned. But he was no longer entirely clear about who it was he wished the damnation to fall upon. He only knew that he was tired and cold and had to keep on.

Chapter 21

He fell again, the chill of the water shocking him out of his stupor and bringing him awake with a startled cry. The water poured into his mouth when he opened it to yell, and he scrambled upright, spitting and gasping.

He had been walking in a semiconscious state for . . . he had no idea how long it had been, only that he had been moving blindly for some time now.

He dimly remembered the creek he was following joining with another, larger stream at a juncture where two small canyons became one larger one. That had been . . . he blinked and tried to look upstream, but he could not see. Somehow the afternoon had slipped away from him. It was dusk already, and the shadows were deep in the canyon bottoms. From where he was now he could not tell where the two small canyons joined to form this one where he now walked.

It occurred to him with no particular sense of alarm that he was walking now between banks that were bare of vegetation, just near-flat expanses of gravel and rock that were scoured free of growth annually during the highwater snowmelt season.

He had no idea how long or how far it had been since he had left the protection of the leafy growth along that first small creek.

He knew he should be frightened by that. He knew he could not hide here on this flat of water and gravel. But he could not work up any interest in being frightened just now.

He knew he should be cold too. He was drenched again, soaked by the water he had fallen into, his shirt and trousers clinging to his skin. But he was not particularly cold. If anything, he felt only numb and oddly detached from the fear, the cold, the hunger, the weakness . . . from all the things that had been haunting him of late.

He felt light-headed but actually quite cheerful, everything considered. It was nice not to be worried or afraid any longer. Drayne smiled to himself and began to hum an ancient cradle tune that he had not heard or thought of in years. The sound of it was soothing and nice, and he hummed a bit louder, becoming proud of himself to realize that he could remember the notes after all the years. He tried to take a step forward, to continue on down the stream as he had been, and discovered that he was not standing. He was kneeling in the water where he had fallen. Off balance, he started to topple forward, caught himself with his hands, and crawled out of the water instead. There was some reason why he was supposed to remain in the water, but he could not remember what that reason had been. Or if it still applied.

The sharp bits of gravel hurt his palms, and he tried to get to his feet, lost his balance, and sprawled face-down onto the bank. Only his feet were still in the water, though, and he was not at all cold now. He laughed. Tried to hum the old song again but could not recall now how it went. Not that it mattered. Nothing mattered particularly. He felt fine now. Quite fine indeed. He giggled and crawled further up the bank. Sleep would be nice now. It was almost dark now. Surely no one would mind if he lay down and took a little nap. He might even crawl into that house over there and see if there was a bed he could lie in.

It did not particularly amaze or excite him to see a house in front of him.

Not a house, exactly. Not even what he would have called a shack back home. More like a hole chopped out of the ground, roofed with grassy sod and a log wall and door erected at the front. But he recognized it for a dwelling of sorts and crawled toward it stubbornly and without fear.

The man Bryan Drayne had never heard the term *line*

shack and was not now capable of fearing the presence of a man-made dugout in the midst of what he considered a barren wilderness. But he could recognize the implicit safety of a roof and door and crawled toward them with blind, nearly instinctive determination.

He made it to the door on hands and knees, but deeply ingrained habit forced him to clutch at the frame and use it to pull himself erect, leaning heavily against the front wall to help support himself.

He knocked hesitantly on the log slabs of the door. The door sagged open at his touch. He blinked and waited for someone to answer his knock.

No one came. After a time . . . he had no idea how long he had been standing there propped against the rough logs of the wall . . . he pushed the door the rest of the way open and staggered inside.

The place was empty and nearly dark. Moving mostly by feel, he found the sheetmetal stove that was placed against the dirt back wall of the line shack. Wood for a fire was laid and ready to light, the door of the stove left standing open. Nesting mice had added to the light tinder already placed there.

Drayne fumbled in his pockets to find his box of matches, took one out, and struck it with some difficulty. His fingers were numb, although he could not remember why that should be so.

The match failed to light, and he stared at it dumbly. After a moment his mouth gaped and twisted, and he began to weep. The match was sodden and useless. So were all the others in the box. He remembered now that he had been in the water. He was dressed. He should not have been swimming in his clothes. They would be very angry with him for getting his clothes wet.

He dropped the box of matches onto the floor and felt around beside the stove for the other matches that he was sure should be there.

They were.

He struck one and touched the burning match head to the tinder. The dry wood caught quickly and sprang into a swift, leaping blaze that spread heat through the snug dugout. The metal of the stove creaked and snapped as it warmed. Drayne became aware of how wet and cold he still was and stood for a while beside the stove, turning slowly to warm himself.

Light from the open stove door filled the interior of the tiny dugout, revealing a pair of rope-sprung bunks in the front corners of the place, shelves that held tin pails with metal covers over them, tinware plates and forks and spoons. It all seemed perfectly ordinary and acceptable to him. He knew that he was light-headed and not thinking clearly but was not interested in analyzing his situation or his responses at the moment.

After a bit, as the place became warmer, he remembered that he had been hungry. He did not feel especially hungry now but he was sure that he had been. Probably he should eat.

Then sleep. Certainly he should sleep.

But first he should eat.

He reached for one of the mouseproof tin pails to see what he might have for supper.

Chapter 22

He ate several times through the night, slept, woke to eat again. The first several meals were quite uncomfortable. After being so long without food, the dried meat he ate first ran straight through his system and gave him a sudden and painful attack of diarrhea that sent him stumbling outside in search of the backhouse.

After that, though, the hunger pangs that had been virtually absent for the last several days came back full force and he ate until he was bursting, only to wake again an hour or so later with the hunger returned.

The combination of sleep and food gave strength, and a sense of warmth, beyond anything he had hoped for.

Off and on through the night he investigated the line shack and the things that had been left there by the cattlemen. A week ago, Drayne would have considered the cast-off or forgotten items in the cabin just so much pitiful trash. Now those articles were a treasure trove beyond value.

The mattresses for the two bunks had been emptied of their straw or grass or pine-needle stuffing, but the empty tickings of striped cloth had been left behind.

One of these, doubled inside itself and with holes out for arms and head, would provide a reasonably serviceable coat when stuffed with pine needles or grass. The other, left mostly intact, would make a fine if lightweight covering for sleeping.

There were two boxes of matches to replace the one he had ruined in the creek. And candles. There was a mouseproof tin box of wax candles. One he burned almost completely, dripping the hot wax over the outside of a matchbox to make that reserve supply of matches more or less proof against another accidental immersion. The rest he could carry with him.

There was a kitchen knife. Old and with a cracked handle and a blade thinned and weakened from years of sharpening. But infinitely longer and sharper and more useful than his own folding pen-nib blade.

Best of all there was food.

Lordy, but there was food.

Near half a gallon of dried meat ready for consumption. Several gallons of dried beans. Those would require heat and water and considerable time to be made palatable. But he could take some along. And there was dried corn in another container. Dried corn was nearly a staple. He used a coffee grinder he found on a shelf near the stove to reduce several quarts of the corn to a crude meal that he could eat dry if he head to, or cook into a gruel or mush if he had fire and water available.

Several items of canned goods had been left in the empty dugout also, but those had bulged and several ruptured from periods of freezing, and he did not trust them, although his mouth watered at the thought of the tomatoes and peaches they had once preserved.

He kept the fire roaring in the sheetmetal stove, ate frequently, and napped briefly through the night while he prepared a bundle he could carry with him come morning.

It would have been wonderful, absolutely idyllic, to be able to remain here for several days with heat and shelter and food available. It would also have been suicidal. The vigilantes were entirely too close. He had no illusions about how much time he might have gained on them with his simple deceptions. He had to move on, and quickly.

But this crude, abandoned little dwelling just might have been his salvation.

Near dawn Drayne's mouth twisted into a tight, wry smile. The men who sought to kill him just may have saved him. Except for their interference, except for their unexpected gunshots, he would never have come down into this canyon and discovered the dugout. He had thought the country a complete wilderness, isolated and empty. But if there was one such place as this here, there might well be others. Now he knew to search for them.

He ate a little more and pondered, sleepy-eyed and tired but no longer exhausted, with hope as well as strength restored now.

Those gunshots had come from in front of him. They had gotten ahead of him somehow. Had he made a mistake trying to flee in a straight line? That could be it. He had been striking west consistently since he left the way station. They may have noted that and used his own inflexible, unthinking determination to jump in front of him.

No more of that, then. Tomorrow he would vary his line of march.

If he remembered correctly—Lord, but so much of it remained unclear in his thoughts—he must have entered this canyon somewhere to the south of where he was now. And tomorrow the vigilantes would be expecting him to continue westward. They were probably searching now to the south and would anticipate his flight to the west. So tomorrow he would go north instead. Go north perhaps for the whole day. Then west again. Always west. That was where hope and safety lay. But not again in so straight a line to the west.

He smiled again and lifted a spoonful of bland, crunchily undercooked dried beans to his mouth.

He rubbed his chin. His beard stubble was beginning to itch as it grew out. A shave would have been nice, but whoever owned the dugout had not left a razor behind.

Drayne laughed aloud, the sound of it briefly competing with and drowning out the crackle of the fire in the stove. Last night he had been close to death from starvation and exposure. This morning he was concerned about a shave. The difference was a very, very welcome improvement, he concluded.

He glanced toward the bed but shook his head impatiently. No time for that. It would be light soon. Time now to make up his pack and move again. He smiled.

Chapter 23

"How the hell could we've lost him?" Burris complained.

This time Whelan was careful to make no comment on the obvious fact that it was Burris and not *they* who had gone and lost the killer. If the fool had only let the killer walk up to them . . . but there was no point in belaboring that again. A rehashing would serve no purpose and Tom Whelan's ear still hurt a bit. He still could not get over the notion that that farmer Burris would actually fight with his *hands*, for goodness' sake. He certainly did not want a repeat of such low behavior.

Luke said something about taking another look today, while Lou Kirkland polished off the last of the fritters they had fried for breakfast. Hy had already eaten and was off messing with his and Luke's young horses.

"What I think we should do today," Whelan said, reaching for the coffeepot, "is split up."

The others looked at him with frowns but let him speak.

"We covered this rim all the way over to the knob pretty good last night," Whelan went on. "Although I expect it could use another going-over again fresh. But my money's on the canyon down below. I been thinking about it. He coulda got down there without us seeing him. If he did, he'll have left some marks. I'll climb down and look. Meantime, I think somebody ought to go back and find the rest of the crowd. Bring up the dogs to pick him up down below if he done what I think. Let the dogs take it as far as they can an' then we jump west again." He hesitated. "What do you boys think?"

"He's wounded," Burris said, still stubbornly convinced of his own marksmanship after the show of blood on the rocks. "He couldn't have gotten far."

"In which case we'll find him directly and have him in hand, dead or alive, time the rest of the posse gets here."

Burris grunted an acknowledgment of that logic.

"The dogs are for a just-in-case kinda thing. If we get him quicker, why, it still makes it easy for us to all ride back together."

Burris nodded.

"Who do you figure should go back after the colonel and the others?" Lou asked.

"Luke and Hy," Whelan said quickly. "If he went down into the canyon, we'll have to try and get down that chute over toward the point. Their ponies are skittish. No sense in asking that kinda work of them unless we have to." He thought Luke looked relieved. They had all seen the only place where a rider might attempt the canyon wall, and it was not the sort of slide that a man on a green horse would look forward to. Although bad as it was, it was a possibility. This time the killer had not been able to pick his spot, so they would have a chance to close on him if he was still running and not holed up wounded or dead someplace close by.

Whelan sighed. The choice of Luke and Hy to ride back and bring the dogs on was an entirely sensible one. But it was not what he *wanted* to do, damn it.

What he truly would have wanted would have been to get shut of Roger Burris for a while. But sending Burris off after the fuss yesterday would have looked too much like a personal decision and not a sensible one. Which it would have been, damn it. Which it would have been. He finished his coffee and tossed the grounds aside, then began to build himself a smoke.

"There's something I want to know before we take a step out o' this camp," Burris announced just as Luke was getting up to go tell his brother what they were doing.

"What's that, Roger?" Kirkland asked.

"I still say the man's close. He's got lead in him. Couldn't have gone far."

"So?"

"So what do we do when we find him? I mean, Mr. Whelan here crawled right down my throat yesterday for doing what I thought we was supposed to be out here to do, which was to shoot the sonofabitch. My question is, if I see him again and shoot him again, am I going to get jumped from behind again for doing what I thought was my bounden duty?" Burris just was not willing to let it lie. He was speaking to Lou but was looking straight at Whelan.

Kirkland coughed and shuffled his feet in the dirt by the fire. Luke turned away and headed toward the horses. Although if another tussle broke out he and Hy would be quick enough to come watch.

Whelan met the challenge in Burris's eyes with a steady stare of his own but was careful to keep his voice mild. "You want hard-and-fast rules, Mr. Burris? I can't give you any. If a man shoots at you, you just naturally got to shoot back. That's only right. But near as we could see yesterday, this ol' boy isn't armed. He for sure isn't carrying any rifle or shotgun."

"But you can't guarantee me that he don't have a cute little two-shoot derringer in his pocket, can you?"

"No, I cannot. No more than you can say that he does have one."

"But he might," Burris persisted.

"He might," Whelan grudgingly agreed.

He took a closer look at the hint of satisfaction on Roger Burris's face, and for the first time he realized something.

Roger Burris *wanted* a chance to shoot Harry's killer.

Or maybe any-damn-body for that matter.

Roger Burris wanted an excuse to kill a man.

The more Tom Whelan looked at the smug satisfaction that lay in Burris's eyes, the more convinced of that he became.

This was a man from the farm country to the east who

had heard all the wild tales about the used-to-be times and was looking on this posse as his chance to get in on the way things used to be. Riding high, wide, and handsome and shooting it out with desperadoes.

Shee-it, Whelan thought.

Things weren't that way now and never had been. Not really. Not the way those fool stories made out.

And the truth of it, the way things really had been, well, Roger Burris wouldn't be interested in any truths, not that kind of truths, but Tom Whelan had been here to see them and to live through those times, and there was some of it that he didn't like to recall. That part of it hadn't been dashing or gay or romantic. Not no way, it hadn't. Sometimes scary and sometimes ugly but damn sure never romantic the way this Burris was bound to be thinking.

Jesus, this Burris was probably the kind who would actually carve a notch into the buttstock of his carbine if he did get a chance to gun down Harry's killer.

"Something you should remember," Whelan said slowly. "It ain't right to kill a man. That's what we're here about, after all. Because this man we're hunting did wrong when he killed old Harry. We come out here so he could be punished, punished right and proper by the law. We never come out here to do a wrong ourselves."

Burris snorted.

"I know. You don't know what I'm talking about. But you ain't seen the things I've seen, Mr. Burris, and you ain't done the things I've done."

"You're talking about the vigilante-committee business? You told us about that already. I don't see that that changes anything."

Kirkland touched Burris's elbow to stop the newcomer from making a fool of himself. "Tom's had to hunt men before, Roger. That's why I was so glad he came along this time. He used to ride for the Association down in Wyoming."

This time Burris looked at Tom Whelan with a degree of respect and perhaps of wariness as well.

"It isn't something I'm proud of," Whelan said. "I'd rather it was forgotten."

Burris fidgeted, excited now and wanting to hear firsthand some of the stories he would have read about in grossly exaggerated form. "Were you in on that business where they burned the homesteaders alive?" He sounded eager for the details.

Whelan made a face. "That wasn't anything to do with the Association. That was over in Nebraska. And anyway those fellows weren't alive when they were burned. They were hanged first, then somehow the bodies got set on fire."

"But I saw . . ."

"Yeah, I know. I seen those photographs too. But the men were dead before they got burned." He tossed the butt of his cigarette onto the dying coals of the fire and began to build another one. "I'll tell you some of what I've seen, though, Burris. I've seen men hanged without a trial. I've seen a bullet put into a man's breast for pure meanness, just to avoid the nuisance of carrying him to the courts. I've seen things that turned my stomach and sickened me. And I've come to know that you can't turn two wrongs into a right. It don't work that way. And killing a man, any man, is wrong. That's what I've come to know, Mr. Burris."

"How many notches do you have on your gun, Whelan?"

"A man don't carve notches." He could not help adding, "No more than he fights like a cur dog."

"But if you did, how many . . . ?"

Whelan ignored him, concentrating on the flimsy bit of cigarette paper in his fingers, filling and twisting and licking and twisting it again until he was satisfied.

"Come on, Roger. Let's take another scout for the fella you shot," Kirkland said. He looked sorry that he had brought up that business about Whelan's past and gave Tom a look of apology from behind Burris's shoulder so that the newcomer could not see it.

"I'll climb down and take a look in the canyon bottom," Whelan said. "If I find anything, I'll give you a shout. You can bring my horse down with you and meet me there."

He did not want to after all the talking he had just done, but this time, since he was going down that slope alone and Burris just could be right about the killer having a short gun in his pocket, he fetched his Marlin from his saddle and carried it with him when he started down the steep incline.

Chapter 24

Whelan stood and waited for the two men and three horses to come to him. "Over here," he said.

"You've got him?" Burris sounded eager.

Tom shook his head. "Just prints. No man. An' like the old hunter said, man, them footprints make a mighty thin soup."

"What about a blood trail. Is he still leaving a blood trail?"

Again Whelan shook his head. "No sign of any blood. He came off the rim just under where you shot at him and hid in the brush up there. I found where he knelt down by a spring. Left an impression in some mud there, and gravel pushed down into the mud and the weave of the cloth in his britches where he was kneeling by the water. Then he came downstream in the water, but he left a print now and again on the bank. Deliberate, I'd say. You can see over here where he came out of the creek and walked over to the wall right there." He pointed.

"So we got to go up onto the damn rim again? Why'd you have us come down here just to turn around and go back up?" Burris sounded angry. Probably he believed Whelan had just wanted his horse brought down so that he could ride up instead of climbing.

"That's a trail he *wanted* us to find," Whelan said. "It's too plain. That's what made me suspicious at first. He come out of the creek at a flat, muddy place where a body couldn't miss seeing the prints his shoes left."

"Shoes?" Lou asked. This was country where shoes were seldom seen.

"That's right. City kinda things with low heels and

blunt toes. At least I never seen any boots built like that."

"I'll be damned."

Whelan shrugged. "They said he was dressed city."

"I guess you can dress how you want when you're riding a coach through from town to town."

"Anyway, he came out of the creek at a place we'd be sure to see, and he walked over to the cliff there an' made some scrape marks like he was trying to climb and knocked some gravel loose. You can see right there."

Kirkland nodded. Burris did not. Likely Burris did not see the marks that were so plain to Whelan and Kirkland.

"Why d'you think it's a false trail, Tom?"

Whelan smiled. "He left a second trail. Headed back into the creek. Tried to step mostly on rocks, but he messed up here an' there. Right over here"—he pointed again—"you can see part of the impression of a heel. And here he trampled down this onion head. Then downstream he never stepped on the bank again—I'd say he was being careful of that—but he grabbed hold of the brush now and again, like he was trying to keep his balance or something, and broke some small branches. If I had to guess, I'd say he was in pretty bad shape when he come through here but still game and still thinking, trying to put us off."

"How do you know it wasn't some animal that broke those branches?" Burris demanded, staring back toward the cliff. "He's always tried to climb out of trouble before. A deer could've browsed those branches."

"It wasn't a deer," Whelan said, trying to hold back his irritation. There was a world of difference between what a browsing deer would do and what a man would leave behind, but he had no intention of getting into that with Roger Burris.

"So you say he went downstream?"

"Yeah."

"He could've slipped back upstream and be hiding along the creek someplace," Burris said, still clinging to the idea that the killer was badly wounded by his bullet, blood trail or no blood trail down here.

"I searched the bottom while I was waiting on you to bring the horses down. He isn't behind us, and he's had all night and half of today to get ahead of us. But I don't think he'll have been moving too fast. The way he was grabbing on to things for support, I'd say he's pretty much done in."

"Wounded," Burris said with satisfaction.

"Right." The point was not worth arguing. Hell, it could even be true.

"Do we wait here for the dogs?" Lou asked. "The rest of the boys won't know where to find us if we go off too far ahead."

"I'd say we go ahead and do some looking. We can always slide back here if we miss them. Better yet, we'll post a note to tell them we've gone on. You got your tally book in your saddle pockets, Lou?"

"Book and pencil, like always."

"Then write it out and stick it on a branch or someplace where they'll see."

They left the message and rode downstream, leaving the small canyon branch a mile or so later and going into a larger, wider cut coming off the finger rims above.

"Which way now?" Burris asked. They were standing at the juncture of the creek they had been following with a large stream flowing through the main canyon.

"Flip a coin," Whelan suggested. There was no brush close on the banks of this larger stream where they could look for the signs they had been able to follow this far. Here the spring floods caused by the snow runoff of several feeder creeks scoured the flat banks free of permanent vegetation for a good thirty or forty yards on either side of the now-innocent creek.

Kirkland was hanging back a few yards, standing in his stirrups and looking south, then north, then back again into the small canyon they had just left.

"Y'know, Tom, this country looks familiar to me for

some reason. I'd almost swear I've been here before."

"This is a ways off from your normal range."

"Yeah I know, but it sure looks familiar when I see it from down here. Didn't from back in there, but . . ."

Kirkland snapped his fingers. "I remember. Emil Defarge. You know the man, Tom?"

"Heard of him. Never met him."

"Well, he bought some yearlings off Santwell and Carson one time, and I helped deliver them. I'm pretty sure this is the high end of the country where Defarge summers his cattle. If I'm right, we delivered them downstream from here a ways, and they put us up at a line shack Defarge has a ways north of here. Not too far, I'd say, or I wouldn't recognize the shape of these walls."

Whelan nodded. "If I was a man running afoot with no coat or bedroll, I'd sure be interested in any line camps I come across."

"Exactly."

"We'll take a look. If there's no sign he's been there, it'd likely be safe to assume he went upstream from here intead of down."

Burris looked pleased. "Hell, he might be laying in there waiting for us."

"I hope he is," Whelan said. He meant it. He would be glad when this business was ended and he could go home and forget about it and about Roger Burris.

Kirkland led the way toward the line camp, and for a change they were able to ride at a lope instead of plodding forward one step at a time.

Chapter 25

"He's been here. The sonofabitch has damn sure been here," Burris declared.

"Yeah, he's been here," Whelan agreed. "Burris, I would appreciate it if you would do me one small favor."

"What's that?"

"Uncock that Winchester you're carrying. The thing kinda makes me nervous."

"Oh." Burris let the hammer down carefully to the safety half-cock notch, and Whelan felt a little easier. Burris had come inside with his carbine cocked and held ready. Tom's Marlin was outside slung at his saddle.

Whelan knelt in front of the lightweight stove that had been left in the dugout and felt of the ashes. They were cold except for a kernel of warmth buried deep at the back of the firebox. "He had himself a fire all right. Been out quite a while now, though. And I'd say he ate plenty, judging from those dishes and stuff."

Kirkland was rummaging in the storage tins. "There isn't much left here except some dried beans and some freeze-ruined canned goods. No telling what else might've been left that he took along with him."

"He's provisioned himself, that's for sure."

"No blood though." Burris sounded disappointed.

"No, I don't see any sign of where he might've bandaged himself or anything like that."

Burris sighed. "Maybe I didn't get him so good after all."

Whelan said nothing.

"Where do we go from here, Tom?"

Whelan walked back to the entrance to the dugout

and looked out into the broad canyon, trying to work out what he would have done had he been in the killer's place.

"North," he said after a bit. "He won't have wanted to waste the strength to backtrack and maybe meet us coming after him. So he'll have gone the other way. But not too far, I'd say. The walls over that side of the canyon are pretty old and crumbly. There's some game and cattle trails. So I don't think he'd want to head west again until he thinks he can put us off at another good climbing place. No good trying to track him from here, of course, but I'd say we could figure him to look for places, side canyons or whatever, where he thinks he could find a climbing wall again to lose us at. We find places like that downstream we can look along them for signs he's been there." He paused. "Either of you got a better idea? I'll be pleased to listen if you do."

Lou shook his head. Burris acted like he hadn't heard.

"No guarantees, but I think this is a chance for us to close on him. We can move right along and only stop to look close at the places that seem likely. Better yet, I think there's some weather coming in. If we get some snow out of it, we can pick up his tracks once and follow him to hell if we have to. Won't be any way he could lose us if we get a tracking snow."

Beyond the canyon wall to the west they could see a line of towering gray clouds moving slowly toward them.

It would be cold and probably wet riding if that front carried snow. But nothing beyond what they were all used to at this time every year. And certainly nothing, Whelan reflected, compared with what it would be like for a coatless, city-dressed man on the run afoot. They were closing on him now, and a tracking snow would be the last boost they would need.

"Let's go." They closed the line-shack door carefully behind them, Kirkland taking one last look inside to make sure the remaining food was tightly lidded and mouseproofed against the needs of next year's cow crew or this winter's travelers. Then they mounted and again were able to hit a fast lope down the creek where the killer had been only hours before them.

Chapter 26

The food helped—oh, Lordy, but it did help—but it was not the instant surge of complete recovery that Drayne had hoped.

He was gasping for breath in less than a mile, hurting in every muscle, and now was burdened with the bum's roll he had fashioned from the second mattress ticking and now carried over his shoulder.

He tried to remember where he had seen such arrangements before. It took a minute before he realized that it had been in old photographs of Rebel soldiers in the field. They too had carried their bedding rolled with their few possessions packed inside and the whole rig slung over their shoulders for convenience. It worked. He had to give it that much.

He tried to remember if the more recent and far better photographs published from the fronts in the Philippines and Cuba had shown similar rolls, but try as he might, the memories would not come to him.

Still, trying to remember such incidentals, trying to think about nearly anything at all except his fatigue and need to continue in motion, was better than dwelling on the present. Better a jumbled past than a horrifying present.

The wide canyon he was following swung westward with the natural drainage contours of the land here, and he trudged forward with mindless determination. Along here the canyon walls were high but not sufficiently steep to allow him to throw off the horses and the dogs.

He passed several places where the eastern wall would have been steep enough. He was tempted to scale a cliff there and strike back the way he had come for a few miles. But safety lay to the west. Safety lay in Idaho with the law and courts and extradition and the attorneys who could be influenced by both money and respectability.

And, dammit, he *was* a respectable businessman. His reputation among friends and competitors alike was beyond reproach. But how does a man explain that to a bullet flying out of a coward's ambush?

Unconsciously he rubbed at the small wounds on his right chest where the shotshell pellets had struck him. The injuries no longer hurt particularly. He had smeared them with some grease he found in the dugout, and that had helped, along with the washing he had given them earlier. Still, they were a powerful reminder of the danger he was in.

The men who were chasing him had no interest in justice. Their only desire was for vengeance. And neither reason nor right has any defense against blind vengeance. These people had not waited for explanations. Their responses were base and ugly. An eye for an eye. A tooth for a tooth. A life for a life.

Drayne shuddered and walked on.

In addition to everything else, now he was beginning to limp a little as he tried to relieve the soreness that was developing in his feet. His shoes had become thoroughly soaked when he walked through that creek yesterday, and they had not completely dried overnight. Now he could feel blisters beginning to form where the damp leather chafed his flesh through the scant protection of thin stockings.

Still, he was much better off than he had been. He had eaten. He had a supply of additional food. He had matches and a knife. And he had gotten at least a little rest. Best of all, the makeshift coat he had fashioned from the mattress ticking was a blessing.

The weather was more chill today than it had been, the sun hidden now by a high wall of dark clouds he could see to the west.

He stopped once to drink from the stream, moving slow and shallow here on this nearly flat bottom, and ate a dry handful of the corn he had ground in the coffee mill. The flaky, crunching stuff was barely palatable, and even in his desperate state he had to force himself to eat it, swallowing it with as little chewing as he could get away with and washing it down with water. It was the nourishment he needed, though, and not the flavor.

Flavor was scrod or beefsteak or lobster live in the pot and served with drawn butter. His mouth watered and his stomach wrenched at the thought of the delicacies he had so easily taken for granted in civilized surroundings.

Better not to think about that.

He tried instead to work out where he should have been by now had the incident at the way station not happened. Was he overdue in Seattle? Would anyone have inquired about him?

Probably not. As best he could recall—his itinerary, jotted carefully in a neat, tidy hand, was in his suitcoat along with cash and tickets and letter of credit, along with all the paper things that attested to his character and respectability—he would not have been due there for another four, perhaps five days. The time that would have been required to complete the stagecoach segments of his relaxed journey west.

No one would be expecting him for at least that long, then. And his Seattle appointments had been tentative. He had been oh so careful to specify in his wires that he would be making a vacation of the journey. That the many connections involved could lead to delays. No one would really become alarmed by his failure to meet those appointment dates. Not for a week. Two weeks. Possibly even longer.

The people he was to meet in Seattle were, after all, only business contacts acquired through letter and telegraph at long range. They were not friends, not even acquaintances. He would not have recognized them had they been seated in the way station back there. They might not react at all to his failure to arrive on time, not even with a wire to New York. They might merely shrug and look for other buyers.

So there was no chance of help there.

Help. Had he really been looking for avenues of

assistance? No, he told himself. Just passing the time. Trying not to think about hunger or fatigue or dogs or men with guns.

Just walking.

Just trying not to think at all.

That would be better. Not to think at all would be wonderful. But how does a man *not* think?

Ignorance is bliss? There just might be something profoundly accurate in that old saw.

Drayne plodded forward along the rocky banks of the creek, exposed there but sure he was leaving no tracks for the men behind him to follow. Unless the dogs were on to him already. He caught himself glancing back the way he had come, although there was nothing there to see except barren, empty wilderness and gray, overcast sky.

He probably should return to the streambed and walk in the water again to foil the scent for the dogs. But his feet hurt and he was tired and already he was hungry again, and he simply could not do it. Not right now. Later, perhaps, when he approached a place that looked unscalable. But not right now.

He began humming a Gilbert and Sullivan song. Then stopped abruptly and snapped into an embarrassed silence as he realized that he was moaning rather than humming.

"Oh, Lord," he whispered under his breath, "help me to find a way out of this."

Chapter 27

It was nearly dusk and Drayne was becoming worried. He had not intended to remain on the open, exposed floor of the canyon so long, but he still had not seen a place that looked both steep enough for eluding the vigilantes and yet graded enough for him to climb.

There had been one place, several miles back, that was certainly steep enough. Yet a few hundred yards away, practically beside the cliff that he very nearly climbed before he took the precaution of looking a bit further, there was a deeply cut runoff wash—probably one day to become a branching side canyon in its own right—that was shallow enough for a horse or a man to walk up without having to pause for breath.

The temperature had been falling for much of the afternoon, chilling his exposed fingers—he wished now that there had been some gloves left in the dugout or that he had taken the trouble to fashion some makeshift covering—and sending them through the various stages of cold, from tingle to sting to pain and now, finally, to a dangerous numbness.

If—when—he did find an appropriate face to climb, he would have to be very careful of his hands. A slip and a fall would be absolutely fatal, if not immediately then as soon as the vengeance-ridden vigilantes found him.

He flexed his fingers while he walked, beat his hands against his sides, tried tucking them underneath the bedroll he carried draped over his chest. Nothing seemed to do more than increase his anxiety over his hands.

It looked like it might snow tonight, too, and the thought of snow terrified him. Snow meant footprints.

There would be no question about where he went then. There could be no false, misleading trails laid.

Snow meant death.

He shivered, the chill reaching him through the double layers of ticking cloth. He had not yet filled the dubious garment with pine needles, so as yet it offered him only minimal protection. He would have to do that soon. But first he had to find a place where he could climb out of this canyon but where the pursuers could not easily follow. The canyon would be as sure a trap as a steel-barred cage in a zoo if he allowed himself to be caught in it.

As a last resort, he concluded, if he absolutely had to, he would stay on the canyon floor until dark, then make his way up the west wall wherever the loss of light took him. That would do nothing to foil the dogs, but the country above was more heavily wooded. There would at least be some cover to keep the men with the guns from seeing him easily. The floor of the canyon was simply too open and exposed.

He tried to see the sun to determine how much daylight he had remaining, but he was walking too close to the west wall to judge. He knew the light was fading, but that was all. Shivering and blowing on his hands, he hurried forward, bent and hunched against the cold but craning his head upward, trying to evaluate the steepness of the slopes above his left shoulder.

He was hungry again—it seemed that he was always hungry nowadays—and was anxious to find a place for the night where he could rest and perhaps start a fire to warm himself and to cook a gruel of ground corn and shaved dried meat. The prospect of something hot to eat spurred him into a quicker pace despite the fatigue that constricted and weighed down the large muscles of his legs.

There? Just a little way ahead?

For some time now he had been passing a section of wall that looked steep enough to stop a horse but not a dog. And over there was a rough, rocky face that just might do.

Might have to do, regardless.

He looked up. The light was dimming, although the low, gray clouds scudding above the canyon were partly to blame. The clouds had a threatening appearance, and looking at them made him feel even colder than he already was. He thumped his hands against his chest and flexed his fingers as he broke into a stumbling run toward the base of the cliff. He would have liked something steeper, really. But this one was certainly high enough.

And it would just have to do. He no longer had the privilege of choice. Soon he would not be able to see well enough to judge if he walked past the perfect spot for evasion.

He hitched the bedroll with its invaluable contents of food, knife, and matches higher on his shoulder and began to climb. Easily at first, but the increasing steepness soon made climbing a matter of slow, serious concentration, with each hand and foot hold vital to his safety. Unlike the other, near-solid cliffs of rock he had climbed before, this one was a mixture of rock and loose gravel.

Each step on the steeply angled gravel meant a slip. He learned it the hard way when his right foot slid out from under him on the loose surface. He fell heavily against the slope, the bedroll partially cushioning the shock of the fall, and slid downhill a good dozen feet before he was able to catch himself against a jagged boulder embedded deep in the crumbling gravel soil.

He clung there motionless for a moment, sharp bits of gravel biting into his cheek, until his breathing came under control again and the hard, quick pounding of his heart subsided.

The thrill of the sudden fear he had felt oddly warmed him, but he was shaky and tentative when he started up again. This time he was extremely cautious with each foot placement and tested every handhold before he gave his weight to it.

He climbed again. Slowly now. Traversing back and forth across the face in search of his footholds and to reduce the steepness of his upward motion. It was hard work and he was already tired, but the heady prospect of reaching the top and being able to find a place where he could safely build a fire and cook a supper drove him on. That incentive overcame the fatigue and lent a false strength to his efforts. The nearer he came to the top—to heat and food and rest—the harder he drove himself.

The top was already in sight. Soon in reach.

He no longer felt cold.

This was no time for a misstep and fall, he cautioned himself. He told himself, willed himself, to slow down and be careful. But he continued to scramble for the top as quickly as he could force his body's responses.

"There!"

The sound chilled him, froze him with terror.

The sound came from *below*.

"Up there, Lou. I see him."

He looked down in time to see two horsemen—no, three—close to the base of the cliff. One of the men was standing in his stirrups and held a rifle in his hands. White smoke puffed out of the muzzle, the center of the smoke ball a bright flicker of orange flame in the twilight.

"Oh, God," Drayne groaned.

Somewhere under his feet, but mercifully falling far short, a bullet slashed into the slope and sent a spray of small gravel into the air.

A low, animal moan of anguish burbled deep in Drayne's throat. Fear-frozen muscles thawed and he hurled himself sideways for the protection of a boulder top as now the second man began to shoot at him too.

Small pellets of deadly lead pinged and whined off the mountainside around him, the marksmen adjusting their aim for distance and angle now, and Bryan Drayne curled himself into a tight, fetal ball and covered his head with trembling arms in a futile attempt to ward off the bullets.

Chapter 28

They loped swiftly along the west wall, their progress broken frequently by the need to stop and examine each of the places where Whelan thought the killer might have tried to make for the top.

Invariably Burris took the lead while they were moving, his leggy, slightly nervous brown mare surging ahead of the other horses as if by some right conferred by her breeding, which was undoubtedly higher and hotter than that of the ranch horses Whelan and Kirkland rode.

Lou tried to keep up with the mare's pace, more or less succeeding, and Whelan was content to bring up the rear of their small procession. Yet every time they came to a slope or a rock-jumbled wash that had to be investigated closely, the lead pair had to stop and wait for Whelan to catch up and pass judgment on whether a trail could be found there.

Kirkland was competent to make such judgments but did not choose to do so, doubting his own tracking abilities and unwilling as well to make Tom Whelan think he might be wanting to take control of the party. Burris simply hadn't the knowledge or the experience to see if a fan of spilled gravel had been caused by a frost-heaved rock, a deer's hoof, or the shoe of the fleeing killer.

Burris, Whelan thought unkindly, would require sign-posts and signal flags to mark a trail he was capable of following.

Twice already they had ridden over paths used by elk on their way down to the creek to water, and each time Burris, in the lead, had loped blindly over them. Kirkland had seen them but ignored them, as Tom did himself. Any place shallow enough for an elk to negotiate could be handled as well by a horse, and their man was looking for a steeper escape than that.

Still, they had to be closing on the man.

The killer was keeping to the stone-littered border along the stream so as to leave fewer footprints behind, but he was not particularly skilled in open country.

Even while riding at a lope, swinging a little closer to the creek than Burris and Kirkland did, Whelan could see an occasional shoe-sole imprint between rocks or the places where the man had knelt to drink. Whelan did not bother to mention those signs or stop to examine them. The track he wanted to find now was the track the killer was standing in. The prints did prove, however, that they were on the right line, that the killer was still ahead of them. At the pace they were making they had to be closing on him.

He glanced high and toward the west. It was hard to tell what with the overcast, but there was not much daylight left. An hour, hour and a quarter at the most, and it would be too dark to track any longer.

Perhaps if the colonel and the boys caught up, they could put the dogs onto a night run. But that depended on whether Hy and Luke got back to the canyon with enough day left that they would spot the note and come on.

Maybe, if they hadn't made any progress by nightfall, Whelan thought wistfully, he could send Burris back to locate the rest of the bunch and lead the dogs on. He thought that but knew he would not do it. If anyone had to go, he would either ask Lou to do it or make the night ride himself. He didn't want anyone thinking he was trying to get rid of Roger Burris, dammit. He was stuck with the man's company for the duration of this run, regardless of whatever else happened.

"How 'bout over there?" Lou asked, dropping back enough to make himself heard without having to shout. He pointed toward a low, overhung cliff formed more of soil than rock.

Whelan shook his head. The cliff was a place a man

likely couldn't climb without the benefit of ropes and plenty of assistance, what with that overhung lip at the top. And besides, there was a cow trail coming down the shallower slope right beside it. It was not the sort of place their man would choose.

"Not that one," he called.

Lou nodded and turned his attention ahead toward Burris, who was still cantering along like he hadn't heard.

Whelan frowned.

It was not the sort of place the killer would choose to go up. *Unless this jehu was a whole helluva lot smarter than they had been giving him credit for being.*

Now that was a thing, wasn't it? Whelan asked himself.

The killer was ignorant of the country. That much was pretty plain from the edibles he had walked past when he was hungry. But he wasn't stupid.

The killer learned quick.

They'd jumped ahead of him that one time by seeing that he was running west. But they'd only been able to do it the once. After that the killer quit running straight west and now was moving north. He was apt to wigwag back and forth any old way and still make his way west if that was what he wanted to do, so now it would be damned hard to jump ahead of him like they had that one time. If only Burris hadn't been so quick on the . . .

No point in fretting about if-only's now, Whelan reminded himself. Trying to figure out the killer, that was what counted now.

The guy had spent days leaving them and the dogs at places they couldn't climb up and down. That only meant that was what he *had* done, not necessarily that it was what he was *going* to do. Damn it. The guy just might throw them now by ignoring the rough places and trotting smack up the middle of a cow trail while they were left behind still looking for the kind of places he *used* to use.

"Damn," Whelan told himself aloud.

Without the dogs to keep the killer honest, he could switch tactics on them and slip right away. Run like hell for a stage line that would carry him out of the country and off free and them none the wiser about it. Or hell, he could follow the chain of mountains clear up into Canada from here and stand in the middle of the street and thumb his nose at them if they ever did figure it out and catch up with him.

Whelan shook his head again. Canada was too far for a man afoot to consider. But they weren't so awful far now from Pritchard and Murrey and Beale's Gulch. If he reached one of them and jumped a stage, he was as good as gone. They hadn't a name or so much as a good description to go on if they lost him up here. So, damn it, they were going to have to start looking close at the easy places, not just the rough ones. At least they hadn't yet passed by him. The signs left along the creek proved that. But Whelan was going to have to quit paying attention to annoyances like Burris and put his mind close on business if they wanted to lay hands on Harry's killer.

He reined the roan over to the foot of the cow trail and checked it close. Any prints left behind by Emil Defarge's cattle were long since lost, but some deer and a cat had been down the path lately. Nothing else. No human footprints.

Still, from now on he was going to have to smarten up and pay attention to the obvious places and not only the tough ones, just to make sure the man didn't pull a fast one on them.

Damn it.

"There!"

The sound of Burris's shout reached him, and he saw Kirkland spur forward. Burris had brought his mare to a halt and was dragging his Winchester out of the boot.

"Up there, Lou. I see him."

Whelan threw the steel to his roan. Burris's carbine cracked, the farmer not even taking time to dismount for a steady shot, and Kirkland yanked his rifle out too.

Both of them were busy blowing holes in the mountainside when Whelan dropped off his saddle and ran over to them, his Marlin ready in his hands.

Chapter 29

Whelan got only a glimpse of the killer before the man ducked behind a boulder that was embedded in the side of the steep mountain above them.

So the guy *hadn't* yet figured he could try to run the easy places. He was still worried about the dogs, wherever they were.

Whelan realized the foolishneess of such figuring now that they had the killer trapped. Pointless. They had the man now. All they had to do was wrap him up and carry him home so the law could take its course.

"What the hell are you boys shooting at?" Whelan asked.

Burris and Kirkland were still peppering away at the hillside where the killer had just been, even though there was nothing to be seen.

"The sonofabitch is up there, Tom. We seen him."

"I know. I saw him too. Ducked behind that rock up there. But there's no place he can run to now."

The rock was exposed on the slope, up near the rim but enough short of it that the killer would not be able to make a scramble for the top. He would be in full view all the way with not a thing to hide behind, and the footing up there was slick with loose gravel.

Every time a bullet struck you could see the spray of soil and gravel from it, and a miniature avalanche of loose stuff would slide down. The shooters kept firing until their carbines were empty and then they quickly began to reload. As soon as his magazine was charged with fresh cartridges, Burris began firing again. This time Lou did not join him in the noisy exercise.

"There's nothing up there to catch a ricochet off of," Whelan said calmly.

Not that he particularly gave a damn if Burris wanted to burn some powder. No one was going to be hurt by it. Including the killer.

Burris continued firing until he ran dry again. Then at last he dropped the Winchester to waist level, took a deep breath, and this time reloaded more slowly.

"What d'you think, Tom?"

Whelan shrugged. "I think the man's caught, Lou. All we got to do is bring him down. We'll tie him up and carry him back. Find the rest of the boys and go home. I expect by now the sheriff should'v sent somebody. Likely we'll find them at Harry's place."

Lou nodded.

"I'm not riding double with him," Burris declared.

"I will," Tom said. The roan had never been asked to pack double before, but the horse was plenty tough enough for the job. And more than once Whelan had ridden with a calf over his lap or a fresh-killed deer slung behind the cantle. The animal had never balked at that and should accept a second rider without too much fuss.

"Then I guess we fetch him down, huh?"

"Yeah."

Whelan tipped his hat brim back and looked up the slope. He was trying to work out the best way up and back. His fingers were busy rolling a cigarette. He knew how he would like to handle it. But he was not sure he could make the suggestion without offending Roger Burris.

Kirkland apparently came to the same conclusion about the chore and solved the problem for Whelan.

"Why don't you stand watch down here, Tom? You're the best shot with a rifle, so it's only right you should be the one keeping watch from down here. Then me and Roger can climb up and put the arm on the SOB."

"He could be armed," Burris said darkly. "I think we should stay right here and smoke him out."

It was Kirkland who disagreed. Whelan was grateful to him for it. "That won't work, Roger. Like Tom pointed out, there's no hard rock above him to catch a ricochet, so we can't reach him where he is."

"We could get above him. Shoot down onto him from that rim. He couldn't hide from us then."

"That'd work," Lou said, "except it'd take us too long to find a way up there. Be dark in three-quarters of an hour or thereabouts. If we don't nail him down before it gets dark, he's as good as loose again."

Burris frowned, but there was no arguing with Kirkland's logic. They had the killer. But only if they took him in before he had the protection of the night.

Whelan stepped a few paces closer to the base of the cliff. He could see the scrapes where the man had started up. The footing here was poor, and it must have been a tough climb getting up that high. He had just damn near made it away from them again, Whelan acknowledged.

"Hey! You up there!" He paused, but there was no response.

"You're nailed, mister. You can't get away. Why don't you make this easy for everybody and give yourself up? Come out now. We won't shoot. We'll take you back to town. Then it's between you and the law. I don't say you won't have to answer for what you done. But you'll get a fair trial. Give up an' come on down now."

From far overhead they could hear the distance-thinned voice of the man they'd been hunting.

"I already saw your version of fair. No one bothered to ask what happened. You tried to kill me. You keep trying. I know better than to trust your kind."

Whelan sighed. It was no more than he had expected, really. If only Burris hadn't shot that time, they would have taken the man easily.

Except that was not the truth. Not really. The truth was that if Burris hadn't shot before the man was in range, he would have shot as soon as the man was too close to miss, and the guy would be dead now, not in irons.

That was the real truth of it.

"Give yourself up now, and we won't shoot," Whelan shouted up the mountain. "We'll give you safe conduct to the sheriff. You'll get a fair trial." In a lower voice he added, "You boys start on up. I'll keep him talking if I can."

"What if he's got a gun?" Burris persisted.

"If he's got a gun, he'll have to expose himself to use it. I'll be here covering him. If he shows a gun, I'll shoot him."

"Leave me alone," the distant voice cried. "That man at the stage stop . . . that was an accident. He hit me. I never tried to hurt him."

"Tell that to the sheriff," Whelan shouted back. "You'll stand trial. You can tell your piece then."

"Go away." There was anguish in the voice. Whelan felt sorry for the man. Hell, maybe it had been an accident. He hadn't been there to see what happened. Not that it made any kind of difference right now. Harry was dead; this man killed him, and it would take a court and judge to work out what had to be done next. A little bit of sympathy wasn't going to make Whelan pass the judgment, not for or against.

"We can't do that," Whelan returned. "We just want to see justice done. Give yourself up now and there'll be no harm come to you."

Kirkland and Burris were climbing slowly but steadily, slipping and sliding and cussing under their breath but trying to keep quiet about it. They were still a long way below the place where the killer was hiding. Lou had left his Winchester propped against a rock at the bottom so he would have both hands free for the climb, but Burris was stubbornly hanging on to his and was making slower progress of it.

"You have our word," Whelan shouted. "Throw out your pistol now and show yourself. You won't be harmed." That should make Burris feel a little better about it. If the guy would do it.

Huh. Probably he couldn't do it. Whelan was more than half convinced that the guy wasn't armed. If he was, scared as he sounded now, he'd have tried to shoot back by now. Would have tried to pin them at ground level or anyway slow them up long enough that he could wait for dark and slip away.

A man wouldn't even have to show himself to do that much. Just a loud noise pointed generally downhill would be enough to put the caution in them. A man trapped like this one was would work that out quick enough.

No, if the guy had any sort of gun he'd have used it by now.

"Show yourself with your hands high and empty, mister. You'll get all the chance you want to tell your side."

This time there was no answer.

Lou was only thirty, forty feet below the man now and climbing steadily. Burris was a good ways lower, hampered as he was by the Winchester he was carrying. Both of them were having to be careful; a fall from so high would be as deadly as any gun.

"Stand up," Whelan shouted. "That's all. Just stand up so we can see you ain't armed."

Lou paused, clinging to a narrow lip of stone or hard-pack. Whelan could not tell if he was waiting for Burris to catch up or if he was resting. A climb like that would make a man puff sure enough. The boys would be tired when they got down again.

A few snowflakes began to sift out of the low, gray sky. The visibility was bad enough without that adding to the problem. Whelan was glad it hadn't started snowing any earlier, though, or they might not have spotted the guy up there. The clouds were so low they looked like they would come down and surround the boulder the killer was hiding behind.

"Give it up now," Tom shouted.

Lou had begun moving up again, Burris still well below him, so he must have just been resting. Whelan knew it was unlikely he could shout loud enough to cover the sounds Lou would be making up there, but he wanted to try.

"We won't hurt you. Give yourself up."

There was a hint of movement at the top of the

boulder, and then the top of the guy's head showed.

"It's all right," Tom encouraged. "Just stand up."

The rest of the guy's head showed as he peered down the mountainside. Whelan waved, wanting the killer to concentrate on him, not on Lou and Burris. He was careful not to raise his Marlin or do anything that could be interpreted as threatening.

"Hold your hands wide so we can see they're empty."

The man looked at him for a moment, then straightened some so that he was exposed from his chest up. He raised his arms.

"No!" Whelan shouted.

Not at the killer. At that fool Burris.

From down where he was, he must not have been able to see the killer until the guy straightened that last little bit.

Now he could. And he was coming up with that damn Winchester.

"Burris. Don't!"

The killer's attention swung from Whelan to the men on the slope below him.

Roger Burris's carbine roared.

Chapter 30

Oh, God!

Drayne threw himself down onto the rock that had been sheltering him, and the rifle bullet smashed into the front of the boulder, then bounced off and struck the slope just above him. Flying rock chips and gravel sprayed his neck and shoulders, stinging sharply, probably drawing blood.

They'd done it again.

Tried to get him out into the open so they could shoot him down.

Tried to? They did it.

Lying bastards!

Tease and promise and play. And kill. Once the playing was over, kill. Like small boys poking sticks at a sewer rat.

Play with it.

Then kill it.

He felt his stomach clench and churn.

The rifle boomed again, and more chips flew. If he had a gun he would kill them. Never in all his life had Bryan Drayne ever wanted to kill any one or any thing. These men he would shoot if he could, by God.

The rifle roared, and gravel sprayed just over his head.

"No. No!"

The protest ripped out of Drayne's throat, the sounds echoed by another voice somewhere below.

"Damn you. Damn you." He was so angry—and so frightened—that his face was twisting into sobbing anguish. He was crying now. He knew that he was. *He wanted to kill them.*

His fingers worked frantically, blindly, searching the ground beneath him in that tiny pocket of shelter behind the boulder. Gravel was piled up there where it had slid the few feet from the rim above. Gravel and small stones. A few larger stones.

Blindly, scarcely knowing what he was doing, not really caring but knowing only that he had to do something, anything, he grabbed at the stones under his body and began flinging them down toward where the men were. He grunted with effort and began to emit a keening sound as he grabbed and threw, grabbed and threw.

"Hey!"

The yelp of protest from below sounded close.

They were going to kill him.

And startled.

They were murderers.

"Don't."

Kill him if they could.

Not that easy, they wouldn't. Not climb up here and shoot him like a broken-legged cart horse being put out of its misery on the street.

Not that easy.

He was panting with exertion and with fear and with the tears that were pouring down his cheeks, but he continued to grab up anything he could move and fling it down toward the men who lied and betrayed and wanted only to kill.

There was another yelp and then a scream. Drayne grabbed up another stone and looked over the edge of the boulder. One of the men had lost his balance, the one with the rifle, and was sliding and twisting out of control down the loose gravel of the slope. The other, the nearer one, was staring up at him. That one had a gash in his forehead that was beginning to flow bright blood. Bright, *satisfying* blood.

Drayne wanted these men to bleed.

He wanted them to die.

He wanted them to go away and leave him alone.

With a scream that mingled defiance and terror, he raised the stone in his hand and flung it down toward the bleeding, upturned face of the man who was clinging precariously to the mountainside. The stone struck short of the man and bounced, striking another, larger rock and starting a small slide of rock and gravel.

The man's eyes widened as the avalanche of stone began over his head and swept down the slope, obscuring him in flowing earth and rising dust so that for a moment Drayne could not see.

There was another scream, loud and close, and the man was swept off his toehold on the mountainside and fell free for an instant, struck the slightly angled slope, and twisted, his fall starting another and larger slide that carried him downward with dizzying speed. The man's arms and legs flailed as he rolled out of control on the tide of moving gravel. He reached out for a rock, hooked an arm over it, but was caught short for only the briefest eye blink of a moment as his sudden weight ripped the rock off of its bed of gravel and sent man and stone alike back into the wave of the avalanche.

The body was sliding limp now, turning and rolling with the whims of the flowing gravel, until it reached a small projection and slid over, losing contact with the mountainside, falling free, arms and legs loose and floppy. It struck hard atop a huge knob of sharp rock buried near the base of the cliff.

The body lay sickeningly still, and Drayne's gorge wrenched and heaved as he tried to keep himself from puking at the finality of awful impact.

Drayne blinked. He felt disoriented. Foggy. The way a man will when he is suddenly snapped awake from a particularly gruesome nightmare. He looked blankly down at his hands. They were dusty and dirty and abraded from his frantic clutching for the stones.

No one was shooting at him. He wondered for a moment why they were not shooting at him. He could see all three. The one that had fallen first was near the bottom, lying with one leg twisted at a freakish, unnatural angle. The one that Drayne watched fall was motionless on the stone knob where he had finally come to rest. He had to be dead. Drayne was sure of that. The man was most surely dead from the fall.

The third one . . . he had been rushing up the slope toward the first. Now he had stopped. He was poised between the two others. Looking quickly from one to the other as if uncertain which of them he should run to. The live one or the dead.

Unaccountably, Drayne began to giggle.

And he began to cry again.

None of them seemed to have rifles in their hands now. The one that had stayed on the ground had left his weapon behind when he tried to climb up and help the others. The other two must have lost theirs when they fell.

Drayne tore his eyes from the awful scene below. They were not shooting at him now. It was nearly dark. He could get away from them now.

He turned his head and gazed blankly up toward the top of the cliff he had been scaling. The top was only moments away.

Safety was only moments away.

A light snow was sifting out of the near-dark sky. Funny that he had not noticed that before. It was already beginning to collect on the ground, but he had been so afraid, so panicked, that he had not even noticed the snow until this moment.

Snow meant they would be able to track him.

But not until tomorrow.

Those sonsofbitches would do no tracking until tomorrow. And he had all night to run through the falling snow. Falling snow that would *cover* his footprints until they resumed their tracking and got close enough to him to find fresh-made footprints.

He turned away from the dead and the injured and the angry and began, carefully, to climb those last few yards to the top of the cliff and the hope of safety.

Chapter 31

The hell with that asshole Roger Burris.

Whelan had started up the slope to see if he could help when Burris lost his balance and started sliding. Then the killer began throwing rocks—throwing *rocks*, for God's sake—and Lou came crashing down.

Whelan ended up caught between them, Burris ten or fifteen yards upslope, lying there moaning and groaning and acting like the damned fool he was, and Lou wound up at the bottom, lying on top of that rock outcrop and looking like he'd been squashed flat. He'd looked and sounded dead when he hit.

But Tom had to find out for sure.

Burris could wait. If he was doing some suffering while he waited, so much the better. He'd gone and shot at a man who was trying to give himself up. If there was any chance to help Lou now—not that he thought there really was one—that had to come first.

Whelan turned away from Burris's pleas for help and half jumped, half slid back down the way he had just come, his boots skidding on the loose gravel so that he completed the short trip to the ground on his rump but in such a hurry that he didn't care or really bother to notice.

He ran to the sharp chunk of rock where Kirkland lay, then had to race around to the other side so he could find some footholds and climb up onto the top of the thing. It was taller than it had appeared, a good eight or nine feet high and half buried in gravel that had slid off the mountain in the years past.

"Lou? Are you . . . are you all right, Lou?"

It sounded stupid to him even as he asked it. But it

was the only thing he could think of to say. He already knew the answer, of course. There truly hadn't been much of a question about it.

Whelan crawled on top of the rock and sat beside Lou Kirkland's body. Lou wasn't all right and never would be again. Or maybe a better way of thinking about it was that he was beyond being not all right.

His eyes were open, the dust of the slide settling on his eyes and dulling them. His face was sticky with dirt-clotted blood, and his mouth was open. The side of his skull was mushy and misshapen. He must have hit something—a rock, a root, anything—at some time during the fall. Tom was almost sure he had been dead when he hit the rock. The sound of him striking had been like that of a beefsteak dropped onto a stone floor. Just so much limp, bloody meat contacting an immovable object. He hadn't even bounced when he hit.

Whelan looked at him for a moment, filled with regret and sorrow and anger and he didn't know what all else.

Filled. That just about covered it.

He hesitated for a moment, then reached out and drew Lou's unseeing eyes closed. Up above Burris was still calling out his name.

"Whelan? Whelan! My God, man, you got to help me. My leg's broke. You got to help me get down from here, Whelan."

The man sounded as much scared as he was hurt.

Tom glanced once more toward his dead friend, then slowly and painfully crawled back down to the ground, leaving Lou's body where it was. There was nothing he could do for Kirkland now that would matter. But he'd had to make sure.

He resumed his climb toward Burris, slower now. He felt very tired. If only Burris . . . If only. That again. If only—if only—if only! He was tired of if-only. Sick to death of if-only.

Jesus!

The snow was falling heavier now, and it would be dark in another few minutes.

He was thinking. Planning. He would have to splint

Burris's leg for him. No sense in trying to set it yet. Not while he was lying up there on the unstable slope where another slide could get started if they weren't careful. So he would have to get the leg in a splint where the man was, then get him down the rest of the way without any more injury, if that was possible. Build a fire, of course, and get some food cooking. Burris would need coffee and a hot meal to help him through the night. The pain would be bad enough without maybe adding shock to their problems.

Build up a ripsnorter of a fire, he was thinking, to help guide the posse in if they'd started down-canyon already. If they hadn't found the note and started through the canyon by now, they wouldn't set off after dark, but if they were already in and moving, they just might keep coming. Tom hoped they would.

He didn't really want to spend the night alone with a live Roger Burris and a dead Lou Kirkland.

He really did not want to do that.

Still, he would do what he damn well had to. That was the only way a man could get along in this world. Meet what came and find a way to get through it.

Still, if only this ignorant sonofabitch hadn't taken that shot at the first sign of the killer.

Whelan stopped and stared up toward the dark sky, into the slanting drift of the snow.

Killer, indeed, that one was.

Burris hadn't any call to shoot this time—and likely nobody ever would really know if Burris was really scared that the guy had a short gun on him or if Burris just wanted to put a notch in his own gun; for sure Burris would never admit to that . . . But now that man up there had gone and killed Lou too.

Just whose fault that had been . . . that was for someone else to work out. The fact remained. Lou Kirkland was dead. Harry was dead. That man up there had killed them both.

For the first time Tom Whelan felt a personal interest in catching that sonofabitch.

"Whelan?"

"I'm coming, Burris. Don't try and move anything. I'm coming."

He started up the slope again.

Chapter 32

Drayne ran. It was much too dark for him to see where he was going or to pick his footing, but he ran.

The slight accumulation of snow already made the going slick over stone, and the ground surface was uneven. He fell frequently, scrambled back to his feet, and ran again.

They were behind him. There had been three; now there were two, but they were right there behind him. They had guns and they wanted to kill him.

He ran.

Chest heaving in the cold, thin air, heart pounding, limbs aching, he ran.

Snow melted on his hair and face, and the chill water ran down his neck and under the collar of his soiled shirt, soaking him beneath the thin covering of the makeshift coat.

After a time—it could have been an hour; it could have been ten minutes—he began to worry and to slow down. The last thing he needed now was anything that would disable or slow him.

He slowed to a walk, then stopped, bending over at the waist and leaning his palms on his knees while he sucked the cold, damp air deep into straining lungs.

There was no sound or pursuit behind him now.

And no sound of baying dogs.

It occurred to him for the first time that there had been only three men on horseback. The dogs had not been with them. The men could have been riding out ahead of the pack, or they could have been a separate party altogether. That could mean that there was more than one vigilante group chasing him. The group with the dog pack and now these riders. The presence of two implied the possibility of even more that he could not know about.

The entire countryside could well be up in arms against him.

Even ahead? To the west? Obviously they knew by now that he was trying to escape west. He would have to change his planning still further. Go north, perhaps, instead of west to try and reach the safety of civilization.

He tried to remember whether he would cross major traffic arteries to the north. Did the upper reaches of the Missouri extend into Idaho? He did not think so but could not really remember. In his case loaded on the rack of that coach he had had a map. Fat lot of good that did him now. Or railroads. Where did the railroads run in this country? He could not begin to recall. Such information had not seemed important to a traveler who was avoiding the rails in favor of the romance of coach-and-four. Some romance.

Drayne was tired. He had been shot. There were men not far away who would kill him as readily as he would dispatch an ant on the dining-room floor. He hurt and he was hungry and thirsty and absolutely stank from going so long without bathing. He had not shaved in days, and his beard stubble was beginning to itch and irritate.

After a bit he straightened, bending backward from the waist to stretch tired muscles, and shifted the bedroll on his shoulder.

The snow continued to sift out of the unseen clouds, making it impossible for him to see anything.

He grunted softly to himself. If he could not see, neither could they. Wherever they were, however close or far, they would be able to see not a whit better than he.

That was an advantage if he chose to make use of it.

Bryan Drayne had too few advantages to ignore any of the few.

At least for now the dogs were not with them, and if they were following, they were doing it as blindly as he in this snowy night.

His sense of direction was uncertain at best in this

hostile country; he depended on the sun alone to find his way. Now he had no clues as to direction. Nothing except the knowledge that when he breasted the top of the fatal slope behind him he had been facing generally west. He had continued to run in as straight a line west as he could manage.

But now they were expecting him to continue on that way, and they had no dogs with them to detect any deviation from the pattern. And as long as the snow continued to fall, the flakes would build over and cover the footprints he left behind him. Any tracks he left right now would be obscured. It would only be later, when the snow quit and left a clean blanket of undisturbed white behind, that he would be endangered by that.

So now was the time to evade them.

He stood and made a quarter turn to his right so that he was—presumably—facing north.

Drayne permitted himself a small smile. He started off again, at a slower but steady pace this time and in a direction at right angles to the one he had followed so far.

Without stopping, he fumbled inside the rolled mattress ticking that was his bedroll and found the ground, dried corn he had prepared back at the dugout. He ate it uncooked as he walked, forcing himself to ingest it slowly and only after allowing it time to soften from his saliva before he swallowed. After each mouthful of the gritty, unpleasant stuff, he bent and scooped up a handful of snow, which he melted in his mouth and then swallowed.

At some time during the long night a curious sense of optimism, almost of euphoria, filled him. The feeling puzzled him but would not go away, and he thought about it as he walked.

Eventually he sorted it out.

He was endangered, yes, by deliberate pursuers who would kill him if they could. But he had food and water now and the promise of warmth when he stopped. He was in a reasonably good state of health and strength thanks to the stop at the dugout. Most of all he was *free.*

He was—the realization was incredible but undeniable—actually quite *happy*.

Tomorrow he could quite possibly die a felon's death, but tonight, *at this particular moment in time,* he was free and he was happy.

He tried but could not remember ever before experiencing anything like this odd sense of pleasure. Nothing ever given, nothing ever gained, had produced anything like this feeling. And over such simple things as food and freedom.

Incredible!

He raised his wet, cold face into the falling snow and laughed out loud into the emptiness of the mountain night.

Incredible.

Chapter 33

The return of sunlight at dawn was so indistinct behind the heavy veils of cloud and snow as to be almost unnoticable. Black turned to charcoal shades and those to gray, and that was as far as it went. The landscape as far as Drayne could see was a monochrome of darker or paler gray like a photograph damaged in the development process.

He was immeasurably tired now, and the euphoria he had felt through the night had dissipated with the return of visibility, as if unwilling to linger for examination in the daylight. His mood, in fact, was cranky and irritable.

He stubbed his toe on a hidden stone and cursed into the silence of the white world around him.

The sound of his own voice was startling, and he realized that the completeness of the snow-blanketed silence was unnerving and oppressive.

He had not really noticed before the small noises of the wilderness. The scrape of one pine needle over another. The flutter of a bird's wing. The light skitter of dislodged pebbles. Now everything was buried in a covering of sound-absorbing snow, and there was no breath of wind to stir the white, heavy branches. He shivered, more from an uncertain sort of fear than from the cold, and hunched his shoulders as he continued to plod forward.

Even the countryside itself was different now. Still hilly and rugged but less precipitously mountainous now. Gentler and more rounded where before it had been raw and jagged. And more heavily wooded here as well.

He shivered again and realized that if the dogs got on to him here, it would be difficult and perhaps impossible to find the steep scarps he needed to slow them.

He had not actually left the mountains. Not yet. But if he broke into a country of plains, he would have no defense whatever against the pursuers. He certainly had not the speed to outrun them in a straight-out race, and if they were to pick up his trail on open ground, he was lost.

He remembered the vast, virtually empty plains on either side during his passage west from St. Louis and the rolling emptiness of eastern Montana seen from the comfort and security of a stagecoach seat. He needed that again. A packet boat, a rail car, a coach. Any conveyance would do. He needed both speed and anonymity. Here he had neither.

Drayne sighed. More immediately he needed rest and warmth. His feet stung from the cold, and his ankles were numbed by it, protected as they were only by thin stockings. The snow had fallen to a depth of five inches or more, and every step covered his nearly exposed ankles in the soft, powdery stuff. Odd how dry the snow was here, though, compared with that back home. The snow he was used to was heavy and wet. This was exceptionally light and mercifully dry.

He pondered that while he walked. Or tried to. His thoughts kept stubbornly returning to the things that he no longer had. To logs placed across the huge, ornamented andirons at the club and roaring with flames. To the brandies and mulled wines served before that massive fireplace. To beefsteak and mutton stews and the smell of a damp overcoat collar on a winter's day.

He forced himself to keep walking, but the pace he was setting now was so slow as to be scarcely worth the effort. This snow was light and its pull against his ankles was slight, but it was incessant. Every placement of one foot ahead of the other had to carry not only his weight but that of the dragging snow as well.

He wanted nothing more than to lie down and sleep.

Just to rest, that was all. If he had been offered the chance to sleep in warmth now and never waken, he would have taken it. To sleep in peaceful, warm comfort would have been worth that to him.

He tried singing to raise his spirits, but that was no help. He was in no mood for the gaiety of song. And he felt foolish as hell about it too. Shy, as if he suspected someone might overhear and laugh at his foolishness.

Humming was no better. He stopped after a few useless bars and talked to himself instead. Nonsensical utterings that carried sound without meaning. It was the sound he wanted, though, and not meaning. The silence around him was leaden.

Now that it was daylight and there was snow on the ground, he realized for the first time that the emptiness of this wilderness was shared. He was not so alone in it as he had thought.

Footprints—hoof- and pad- and pawprints, actually—crisscrossd the fresh snow frequently. Crossing from one tree to another. Emerging from a tiny copse of dense brush and disappearing around hillsides. Seeming to start from nowhere and end nowhere, some of them.

Drayne had not the knowledge to determine what sort of animals left the tracks behind except to realize that most of the impressions were made by small and unthreatening things or less often by large and timid things. He had no idea what sort of creatures might exist here. For that matter, he thought ruefully, he had no idea what sort of creatures existed near New York or along the rugged coastline where he preferred to summer. Wild, furry things existed there, certainly, but his personal experience was limited to those wild things that were also human. Of animals and nature he had no ken.

Most of the tracks he saw were fresh, probably meaning that the animals that made them had been moving at the dawn. He was able to see a few faint, shallow depressions in the surface of the snow. Those would be older tracks nearly covered by the continuing fall through the night.

That was good. That was what he was counting on to

cover his own path laid through the long, cold hours of darkness.

It was a set of just such half-hidden footprints that led him to the cave. He never would have noticed the dark opening behind a screen of thick brush except for the tracks left in the snow by some animal that vacated its shelter sometime within the past few hours.

He stopped, tempted, and looked into the slow-flowing clouds that continued to drop a light snowfall over the country for as far as he could see in any direction.

There was no way he could judge how long the snow would last. Logically he should keep moving as long as he safely could, as long as he could reasonably expect the snow to continue to fall and to cover his footprints behind him, but he should stop and rest, say, two hours before the snow quit. Whenever that might be.

"How the hell am I supposed to know when the snow will quit?" he demanded of the silent, sterile hills.

There was not so much as a puff of breeze for an answer.

It was the heavy feeling in his legs and the lack of feeling in his feet and ankles that made the decision for him.

Right now was a good guess as to when two hours before quitting time came. Right now while there was an animal's den for him to crawl into and a thicket of brush near it, not only to keep prying eyes away from the opening to the hole in the ground but to provide wood for a fire.

He was acutely aware of the matches rolled inside his bedding and of the food that was packed there.

He continued on in the direction he had been following, not deviating from that path until he reached the line of depressions left by the departing animal, then turned and followed those footprints to the mouth of the den.

The place really was not large enough to be considered a cave. Although just how big a hole should be to be properly called a cave Drayne was not sure. He had to drop to his knees to get inside.

As his head and shoulders moved into the shelter, the first protection he had had over his head since he left the dugout, it occurred to him that perhaps the footprints were made not by an animal leaving its den but by one returning to it.

There still could be something inside. Some wild creature like a bear or a catamount.

He had seen nothing threatening in this country except for the threats of man. Come to think of it, he had seen practically nothing living in this country except for the men and dogs and horses that were chasing him, even though there was ample evidence in the snow that animals did exist here.

The hell with it, he decided.

"If you're in there, damn you, move over. You have company."

He heard no growls or snarls, so he crawled the rest of the way inside the tiny cave.

Gratefully he stripped off his bedroll, then turned and went back outside to gather wood for heat and cooking. The cold assaulted him anew once he was outside of the protection of the cave. Logically he knew that the interior of the shelter could have been no warmer than the outside air that entered it. But it had felt warmer nonetheless. Or perhaps it was only the prospect of heat and rest that had lent the cave an impression of relative warmth.

Not that it mattered what the truth of that was.

The truth that counted was that he could build a fire now and remove his shoes to dry them and prepare a hot gruel and . . . best of all . . . he could sleep.

Drayne sighed with pleasurable anticipation as he crawled back inside the cave with an armload of dry wood. The feeling of contentment he had lost with the dawn returned now, and he whistled softly to himself while he built his fire.

He was quite sure now that having survived the night he would survive the day. And a man could not ask much more than that.

Chapter 34

Whelan added wood to the fire and pushed the coffeepot to a better spot over the coals already formed. The camp was comfortable. Rather than trying to move Burris to a sheltered location, Tom had built slanting heat reflectors behind the fire and another behind Burris to form a pocket of warmth in the open, snow-coated bottom of the canyon.

"Could you pour me another cup of that, Tom?" Sometime during the night Burris had shifted from "Mr. Whelan" or just "Whelan" to calling him by his first name. It was not a change Whelan particularly welcomed, but at least for the moment they were stuck with each other.

Burris was well within reach of the pot. Tom had made sure of that when he positioned the fire and bedding and reflectors. But instead of reaching for it himself, he wanted to be waited on. Whelan would have thought it preferrable to go without than to ask another man to fetch and carry for him, but obviously Roger Burris did not see it that way.

Besides, the man did not so much want the waiting on as the reassurance that Whelan was there to call upon. Whelan knew that but still there was a twinge of irritation close to disgust as he moved without comment to do as the man asked. He used a pair of forked sticks to pick the hot pot off the coals and tilt the spout over Burris's cup.

"Thanks."

The SOB really was being just as polite as he knew how. Well, he was just going to have to be disappointed for a spell then. The smiles and the first-naming and the phony politeness were only going to go so far.

Tom stood and looked up toward the steep, gravel slope where Lou had died. The snow was coming down still but not quite as hard as it had been. Stupid to chance that route now, though. He would have to look for an easier way up.

Looking back toward the fire, he glimpsed the snow-covered body of the man who had been his friend.

Last night Tom had dragged Kirkland's body down off the rock where it landed and laid him wrapped in his ground cloth. His bedroll Tom had given to Burris to help pad the broken leg. Burris had twisted and moaned through most of the night, hardly getting any sleep and mostly keeping Tom from getting any too.

No doubt the break did hurt like hell, Tom conceded. It was a nasty one, likely busted in several different places, and Tom had made no effort to set it, just to lash it stiff so the bone ends wouldn't shuffle around and cause more damage when Burris had to be moved. Anyway, by the time Tom reached Burris last evening, the flesh around the break was already swelling so bad an expert probably would not have been able to accomplish a proper setting, and Tom was certainly no expert.

Burris had done plenty of hollering getting him down here and onto the bedrolls, but they hadn't really talked. Tom had been in no mood for it, and Burris must have sensed that.

It was Burris's fault as much as it was anybody's that Lou was dead now. Opening up at the first glimpse of the killer like he'd done. Just wanting to shoot somebody and be able to claim he was the one who'd gunned down Harry's murderer. Tom was convinced of that after the whole night to think about it.

No changing it now, though. No changing any of it.

And the killer was still out there someplace, likely getting farther away with every minute that passed, and looking like he was going to get away free and clear from the deaths of two good men.

One genuinely good man, anyhow. Harry hadn't been

all that good. Hadn't deserved to die, though. Even a man who wasn't a saint had a right to keep breathing and doing as he thought right.

That was one of the things Tom had figured out over the years. Even the worst kind of man does the things he does because he believes himself to be right about it, one way or another. Nobody sets out deliberate to do what he considers wrong. A man who robs a bank tends to think that he needs the money and the bank has plenty to share whether they want to or not. A robber thinks of his victim as being greedy, not right. The other fellow is always the one who's wrong. Always.

And right now Tom Whelan figured that Roger Burris and the killer up above there were both in the wrong. One just about as wrong as the other, although the only one who'd ever be asked to pay for being in the wrong was that killer. Burris hadn't done anything that was *technically* wrong. That was the thing. The technicalities. And technically speaking, it was the murderer who'd killed Lou as well as Harry. Burris had only made a judgment that maybe not everybody else would've made.

Pity there wasn't any law against stupidity, Tom thought.

Or maybe not such a shame after all. Most of the population of the damn countryside would be behind bars if there was that kind of law on the books. A guy named Whelan no exception, Tom decided. He should have . . .

He quit that line of thinking. Should-have was about as useless as if-only.

Tom walked out to check on the horses. They were hobbled and loose on the flat at the bottom of the canyon so they could reach water and graze as they needed. They would keep just fine without tending for a while.

He unstrapped Kirkland's saddlebags and provisions sack from behind Lou's saddle—and wasn't it going to be a nuisance loading Lou onto that thing now that the body'd had time to stiffen—and carried them over beside Burris, snug in his nest of thick bedding.

Burris raised an eyebrow, but Tom ignored the unspoken question and went off along the face of the west canyon wall to find more dead wood and drag it into camp. There was a blowdown at the foot of a deep cut a hundred yards or so off, so he had no trouble making the gather. The stuff was heavy, though, so he saddled his roan and used it and his catch rope to drag wood enough that a man could stay warm for days without having to get more.

"What's all that for?" Burris asked at the third load or so.

"The fire," Tom snapped, deliberately mistaking the intent of the question.

Burris accepted the response, though. Likely, Tom figured, he would be looking on the up side of the possible reasons. Like thinking it was because Tom intended to keep him here until some of the swelling went down and he wouldn't be so mean-miserable uncomfortable going back ahorse. A man with a leg broke as bad as that one was wouldn't be in any hurry to get onto a horse again.

When Tom thought he had enough wood gathered, he got out the folding Swedish saw he carried and began reducing the dry wood to manageable lengths.

It took quite a while, much longer than he really wanted to spend on the chore, but he hadn't much choice about it. While he cut, he kept looking up the canyon, hoping to see the rest of the bunch coming, dogs and all, so that he could turn Burris over to them and get on with what he had to do.

He was determined, though. Whether they showed or not—and for damn sure whether Burris wanted it or not—he was going to do what he had to do.

Finally the camp was put together as best he could manage it. There was food, coffee, wood, and water handy to last Roger Burris a week if need be.

Whelan stood. He hauled his Marlin out and from long habit checked the chamber to see that there was a live cartridge under the hammer.

"Where are you going now?" Burris wanted to know. "Hunting?" He sounded hopeful. And nervous too.

"You could say that."

"Not . . . ?"

"The man killed Harry and now he's killed Lou Kirkland. Got to be held to account for that." He bent and picked up his saddlebags, but instead of carrying them toward his horse, again hobbled and turned loose, he draped them over his shoulder and then his bedroll on top of them. The killer was running afoot and kept finding places to lose them on account of it. If he could run afoot, then by damn Tom Whelan could run him *down* afoot too.

"My God, Tom, you can't mean to leave me here. My leg's broke. I can't move. I can't—"

"You can do what you have to. Same as I'll do what I have to. Besides, you got everything you need, and the rest of the posse will be along any time now. They'll carry you home. By now half of 'em will be looking for excuses to head back anyway. More'n half, I bet. They'll take care of you." He pulled his hat snug on his forehead and tossed aside the butt of the cigarette he had been smoking. "I won't be back by the time they reach you. Mind you tell 'em to leave my horse and saddle be. I'll want them here when I come back."

"But you can't . . ." His words died away into a low moan of anguish. There was no point in him saying more anyway. Whelan was already walking off into the snow with a fluid, seemingly lazy, but very swift stride.

Whelan did not look back.

Chapter 35

Drayne crouched in a thicket of brush near the hilltop, excitement causing his heart to beat wildly and his fingers to tremble.

He was wary, though. He was not going to rush out and expose himself until he was sure.

The road he had seen from a distance was directly below him now—not the wagon road; he had crossed that two days ago, unwilling to trust the people who might be on it or the news they might have sent up it with the stage Drayne should have been on—and near it, nestled in the protection of a grove of tall trees, there was a house. A ranch house complete with outbuildings, barn, corrals.

Smoke curled lazily from the chimney of the house, promising warmth and food. Even coffee, perhaps. Lord, but he had come to miss coffee. And the food he had taken from that dugout ran out early yesterday. He was hungry again.

Funny, though, that he actually felt pretty good. The experience he had suffered in the wilderness had hardened him to deprivation in somewhat the same way the walking had toughened his feet and toned his muscles.

He had been running . . . He tried but could not be sure how many days it had been now. So much of it blended together in his thoughts. There had been that first burst of terror and all the climbing. Then the being shot at and the escape through the snow. Two days and two nights hiding in the little cave, eating and recouping his strength while the snow still lay on the ground. It had occurred to him that a man who was not moving left no tracks.

Then the early snow began to melt, leaving the ground nearly as quickly as it had accumulated, once the clouds cleared and the sun reached it. And that had been . . . three days ago? This was the fourth, yes.

If anything, Drayne felt rather proud of himself now. He had done it.

He had no idea how many miles he had covered since the incident at the way station. More than enough, he was sure, to pass beyond the limits of any reasonable search. He had seen no human since those three men shot at him nor heard any voice but his own in that time.

There was a certain satisfaction involved here that he never would have expected. A satisfaction that he was not going to jeopardize by rushing out now at the first hope of relief.

For the time being he would wait here and watch. Just to make sure there were no mounted bands of vigilantes or packs of dogs in evidence. Not that he thought there possibly could be. Just to make sure.

He let out a slow breath and hunkered inside the protection of his cover.

The distant sound of a screen door slamming on its spring reached him, and a moment later a figure in skirts appeared from behind the house. She was carrying something; he could not see what. She carried the object across the yard to the side of the barn and scattered something from it onto the ground. A flock of chickens rushed to surround her, gabbling and pecking madly at the ground.

Kitchen scraps thrown to the hens, he realized.

Drayne's stomach churned emptily. The thought of those scraps going to a flock of chickens . . .

Still, scraps being discarded meant that a meal was being prepared. He felt in his pockets, trying to remember how much coinage he had there. Certainly enough to pay for a meal.

His hands brushed over the ragged tails of the coat he had fashioned for himself from the mattress ticking, and for the first time in many days he realized how utterly disreputable he would appear to someone who did not know how he had come to this state. Did not know and *dare* not know.

He wondered if he should abandon the bedroll and knife here. Not only were they disreputable looking, they were stolen. Odd that he had not thought of his pilferage in those terms until this moment, until now when he was faced with a return to civilization and safety. At the time it had seemed only a matter of survival. Now, with the prospect of meeting uninvolved strangers immediately before him, the then-necessary act of survival was perceived as a theft. Food, bedding, knife, the tin cup he had cooked in . . . he had taken them without thought when he needed them. Now he was burdened with the realization that he had burgled another's property.

He had never stolen anything before in his lifetime. Excepting a packet of chocolates from his paternal aunt's handbag once when he was seven. Even that had weighed on him until he confessed to her, years later when he was twelve or so, and received her forgiveness.

He wondered if now he would be forced to think of himself as a thief in the future. Or if there might be some manner of untraceable restitution he might make to salve his conscience in the matter. That might be the best if he could work it out. Somehow determine who owned the property and send a generous payment for goods and trouble. Yes, that would do. His lawyers could help him to work out the details to preserve his anonymity.

He smiled. His *business* lawyers could do that. Now that he was so close to safety he realized that he had no intention of identifying himself to the authorities here, in Idaho or wherever he was. If he could just slip away and put the whole thing behind him, ignored if never forgotten, well, that was what he would do.

The smile became wider.

He was seriously concerned at the moment about having to view himself as a thief, yet he felt neither guilt nor remorse about Harry or about the man who had died in pursuit of him. He was feeling quite badly about the loss of a few possessions by some innocent in the matter. But nothing at all about the two men who had died.

He could accuse himself of thievery. But not of murder.

He found that curious and wondered about it while he watched the woman in the distance walk over to a low-railed pen and look inside, then return to the unseen door at the back of the house. The screen door slammed again, and Drayne tasted warm spit as he thought about the meal that was being prepared in there and saliva began to flow in his mouth almost faster than he could swallow it back. The fluid reached his empty stomach and lay sourly uncomfortable there.

There seemed to be no one else on the property. Probably the employees and the men of the family were elsewhere working at whatever work was done on a ranch. Certainly, though, there was no sign of the men who had been chasing him.

Probably the sensible thing would be to wait until the workmen returned for supper. Then he could see for sure that the vigilantes were not among them.

But that would be the sensible thing. Even as he thought it he was rising from his cover and stepping into the open on the hilltop. Beginning to walk down toward the faint road and the promise of the smoke from that chimney.

The nearer he came to the house the faster he moved until he was running in a long, loping stride. He stopped just short of the steps to the front porch and used the palm of his hand to smooth his hair back from his forehead. Then, trembling, he mounted the porch and tapped lightly on the door. He was sweating despite the chill of the afternoon.

Chapter 36

Drayne placed the flat of his hand over the cup and smiled. "Thank you, ma'am, but I'm so full now I can't even hold more of that fine coffee. I do thank you. And you, Mr. McKelty. You've both been terribly kind."

"Glad t' do it, Mr. Drayne. Glad you found us." McKelty pulled out a pipe and tobacco, correctly read the longing in Drayne's eyes, and handed the tobacco pouch to him. "A moment, Mr. Drayne."

McKelty limped out of the room on a leg stiffened years ago, he had said, by a fall from a horse and returned seconds later with an ornately carved and seldom used "Sunday" pipe. He handed it to Drayne and watched the pleasure in the younger man's eyes as Drayne loaded the pipe and took the first immensely satisfying puffs from it.

"One thing I can't understand," McKelty said. "How on earth could y' wander so far off from the stage road?"

Drayne shrugged and tried to look the city fool. That was easy enough. He really was one in so many ways. He gave McKelty a sheepish, boyish grin and said, "I couldn't possibly explain it, sir. If I knew enough to tell you that, the incident should not have happened to begin with, I suspect."

McKelty chuckled, accepting the idea of a city dweller becoming lost.

That was the story Drayne had come up with to explain his lost and bedraggled state. He told them he had been traveling west on the coach—which was true up to a point—and that he had gone for a walk while the driver repaired a loose tire, then could not find his way back to road or wagon.

"And this line shack . . ." McKelty was saying.

"Line shack?"

"You said you come across a dugout where you found them things."

"Oh, yes. I have no idea what a line shack would be, though."

McKelty explained it for him. It made sense, then, that the dugout—or line shack—should have been left in its stocked but semi-abandoned state for the winter.

"You say you've no idea which it could have been, Mr. Drayne?"

"I'm sorry, no." And of course he could not. He could have described the place with some small degree of accuracy but did not dare do so. The dugout, or line shack if the McKeltys preferred, was situated on the other side of the wagon road from here. He could not reasonably claim to have lost the east-west-running road twice, after all.

"Well, nobody minds a winter traveler helping himself to a few vittles." McKelty leaned back in his chair and blew a pair of smoke rings. "That's one o' the reasons they're never quite cleaned out come fall, y' see. Never know when a man might be in need, and in country like this there's few enough places for succor in an emergency. You were lucky." He shook his head. "Sure can't figure, though, whose camp you wandered into."

"I wish I could describe it better. I, um, have been rather distraught over all this, as you might imagine."

No doubt McKelty could *not* understand how even a city dweller could mistake north for west, but he politely nodded as if he could. He could understand panic if not disorientation.

"No matter," he said. "Tomorrow I'll hitch the team and drive you down to Beale's Gulch. There's a connection down to the stage road from there."

"I couldn't ask you to take time away from your work, sir. You've been much too kind already. If the road goes there, I can follow it down." He smiled. "Carefully this time."

"Nonsense. Got to lay in some more supplies anyhow." He blew out a puff of bluish-white smoke and winked at Drayne through it. "The missus always likes an excuse to see the other ladies an' gab, you know."

"Gab, is it? And who is it spends the hours talking in the saloon, Mr. McKelty?" The woman of the house gave McKelty a sharp look, but there was a brightness of teasing in her eyes that belied the tone of voice.

"I really do not wish to put you out," Drayne said.

"No bother, no bother. Glad t' be of help."

Drayne could not help wondering how many of his friends and associates back home would put off a day's work and drive who knows how far simply to assist a ragged, unshaven stranger they had never seen before and were not likely to see again. And for no monetary gain either. They had acted offended when he made the mistake of offering to pay for his meal. He wondered if it would be equally offensive for him to offer payment for the transportation. He wished he knew more about the customs of this odd country, so completely different from anything he had ever known before.

Of course it would be worse to not offer payment when one was expected than to make an offer that could be refused. He decided that come the morning he would ask if he could pay for their trouble.

Mrs. McKelty rose and began clearing the table. "Are you sure you can't finish this last bit of roast, Mr. Drayne? Be a shame to throw it to the dog now."

She pushed the nearly empty platter—it had been far from empty when she brought it to the table, and only the three of them eating from it—and smiled warmly when Drayne relented and slid the crusty end piece onto his plate. He was quite sure nothing he had ever eaten before had come close to the flavor of the simple beef-and-potatoes meal he had been given here. And the coffee! Richer than anything served at the Holland House.

He was already full to groaning but managed to finish

the meat and then allowed Mrs. McKelty to force yet another cup of that fine coffee on him while he finished the pipe the mister had given him.

"When you're done, Mr. Drayne, Mr. McKelty will loan you some of his night things. I'll freshen your clothes . . . no, I'll hear none of that from you now, sir . . . and dry them by the stove overnight. They'll not be ironed, but they'll be clean. And I'll not be taking any dispute from you, sir. Mr. McKelty, off with you now. Bring the striped nightshirt and those carpet slippers you never wear. And you can carry water from the reservoir for the gentleman's bath. Show him where, Mr. McKelty."

It had been the men who talked during the meal, but it was the missus who was in charge now.

"And while you're at it, Mr. McKelty, you can bring your soap and razor too. And mind you don't forget the strop. I think he'll need it more than a bit with all that to scrape off."

"I, uh, was attempting to grow a beard while traveling," Drayne said quickly. That hadn't occurred to him before, but he had decidedly more than a four-day growth of whiskers but was supposed to have been lost only that brief time. He did not want these good people's suspicions aroused against him.

A flush of guilt spread through him. First a thief. Now a liar. He would be glad to put all of this well and truly behind him and return to a world of reason and normalcy where he could once again be the sort of man he was raised to be.

McKelty grunted and left the table, off to perform the errands his wife assigned to him.

A bath, Drayne thought. The prospect of a bath was almost more than he could contemplate. It had been so terribly long since he was clean and shaven and wearing fresh underthings. Those were things he had once taken so casually for granted. Now they were great and rare luxuries to savor.

A full stomach, a pipe of tobacco and now cleanliness. Marvelous.

He smiled and smiled and smiled.

Chapter 37

Beale's Gulch was not large enough to be considered a neighborhood by Drayne's previous standards, much less a town in its own right, but to the McKeltys it was the city, and Mrs. McKelty was aflutter with the opportunity to see other ladies and hear all the things they had to say. She had been so since breakfast, Drayne had observed, and probably long before that she had been busy compiling lists, not only of the things she wanted to remember to buy at the store but even of questions she wanted to ask and month-old gossip-doings, she called it—she wanted to catch up on when she saw this friend or that storekeeper.

The McKeltys lived in an isolation that Drayne found as foreign as everything else about this strange and distant land. But once again he was able to view the differences with a sense of amusement, as a passerby and no longer a participant. That was a change he heartily approved.

He sat in the driving box of McKelty's heavy wagon and practically preened. The feel of clean cloth against a clean body, the sensation of a borrowed coat collar against freshly shaven and slightly tingling cheeks, was remarkable. Thoroughly enjoyable for no more reason than that it was *so*. He felt refreshed and comfortable in ways that he could not remember since before his ordeal with the Montana vigilantes began.

In truth, he realized, he felt better than he could ever consciously remember feeling before.

That was the key, of course. Consciously. He had been clean and well fed and perfectly content for nearly all his life. He simply had not paid attention to those mundane satisfactions. There had been no reason to. Now, having once lost the small pleasures, he was acutely, gratefully aware of them.

He told himself he would never lose this newfound sense of awareness and gratitude. But even as he swore that oath to himself he knew that it was a vow human nature would not allow him to keep. As soon as he returned to a truly normal life, as quickly as he reached Seattle and settled once more into the familiar routines of commerce and normal living, he would begin to forget, to accept comfort and security and lack of danger and to drift back toward the casual acceptance of peace and safety and cleanliness.

The best he could honestly hope for would be for him to remember now and then the experiences he had suffered here.

He sighed loudly, and McKelty looked at him with a raised eyebrow. "Something wrong, Mr. Drayne?"

Drayne grinned at the man. "Not a thing, Mr. McKelty. Thanks to you and your wife, sir. You've been more kind than I would have thought possible."

McKelty grunted and jabbed the stem of his empty pipe between his teeth. "Nothing but our Christian duty, Mr. Drayne. Nothing anybody else wouldn't've done." He looked embarrassed by Drayne's comment and relieved to be able to change the subject as they pulled to a halt and backed skillfully into place at the loading dock of a tall, barnlike building with a sign out front proclaiming it a mercantile.

"This is the place I told you about, Mr. Drayne. No regular passenger service here, but Jess can generally find someone a place on one of the freight wagons. George Moss runs his rigs up here whenever there's enough of a load. Couple times a week mostly. If Jess can't put you up himself until the next freight comes in, he'll know who can."

"Mrs. Blake," Mrs. McKelty put in from behind them. "Mr. Drayne should stay with the Blakes. He would eat better and cheaper too, I daresay, if he boards with the Blakes until Mr. Masters arranges his transportation down."

"I haven't much cash with me—" Drayne began, but McKelty cut him off. The man had refused payment for the drive to town every bit as forcefully as he and his wife refused payment for the food and bed and help they had already given the stranger who appeared at their door.

"We'll work that out," he encouraged. "I'll have a word with Blake and with Jess Masters too." He gave the impression that if necessary he would dig into his own pocket to help Drayne.

Drayne did not know how to take such immediate faith and acceptance. It was beyond anything he had ever heard of before. Indeed, beyond anything he himself would have ever considered doing for a stranger. He resolved to show compassion the next time a panhandler approached him on the streets.

"I don't know how I can thank you enough for—" McKelty cut him short again, pretending not to hear and turning to say something to his wife about not forgetting to buy tobacco.

These were good people, Drayne thought. Even if they did not want to be told so.

He jumped out of the wagon and hurried to help Mrs. McKelty down. Her husband was busy with the team and seemed to think that the lady was capable of fending for herself.

The McKeltys led Drayne inside the store, and the news about him caused a stir of excitement about him. Masters, the proprietor of the principal trade center of Beale's Gulch, seemed to think the occasion called for a holiday, and there was a general exodus toward a nearby saloon to celebrate Drayne's survival. A small crowd gathered quickly as the news spread, and soon Drayne was surrounded by rough-dressed, red-faced men offering drinks and congratulations.

"He was lost, all right. But now the sonofabitch is found." The man who spoke was lean and unshaven. He carried a set of saddlebags over his shoulder and a rifle in his hands.

Chapter 38

Whelan had only swung through here to pick up some supplies. The killer was still scooting north the last Whelan saw of his tracks.

Now here he was. Looking smug as a rat in a rice bin with that damned smile on his face while he let the local folks pet and fuss over him like he was some kind of damned hero instead of the lying sonofabitch he was.

Apparently he had spun some whopper about getting lost.

Whelan felt a coldness knot his belly. Lost described the two good men who were without any future because of this man here.

Whelan could feel the stiffness come through him, the pull of tension in his cheeks and forehead, the hint of cold down deep inside, all the dammed-up, tight-wound senses that would build and build until they burst.

The men in the place were all looking at him now. Looking puzzled and unsure of what was going on all of a sudden. The few who were standing close to the killer had sense enough to move a bit aside so they were out of the way of the stare Tom had fixed on the killer.

Tom took the cigarette out of the corner of his mouth and dropped it into the sawdust on the floor. He hunted around with the toe of his boot to crush the coal of the thing but did not look down to see if he had found it. He did not want to take his eyes off those of the killer.

"Some of you men may remember Harry Fischer and Lou Kirkland," Tom said. He didn't have to speak up. They were all for damn sure paying attention to him now. "This man killed the both of them." He did not raise his voice. There was no need for that. The quiet conviction in his tone was enough.

"He killed Harry in his own relay station an' murdered Lou just this past week while Lou was in a posse of us chasin' him down in the Long Canyon country."

An older man who had come in with the killer and who seemed to be taking special care of him coughed and turned his head away. The rancher looked uncomfortable.

"He's a clever sonofabitch, but I been following him afoot," Tom said. "I come to take him. If there's any objections . . ."

He let the warning lie there, and now the group of men who had been gathered so close around the killer moved quickly out of the way, shifting just about as far away from him as they could get.

Behind the bar the barkeep blinked once, realized he had been left behind by the rest of his friends, and jumped to join them, a half-filled glass of beer still in his hands. He came out from behind the bar, drained off the beer in a gulp, and set it down on the bar carefully, like he didn't want to make any noise doing it.

"You'll stand for both them murders, mister. I figure to see to it," Tom said.

The killer didn't look so damn smug now. He was pale and starting to shake.

The party was over. Now it was time to pay the piper.

Chapter 39

Jesus God, they'd found him even here.

This was one of the men who wanted to kill him.

He had done nothing, yet they wanted to take his life.

Bryan Drayne never in his life wanted to hurt anybody, yet they would kill him.

He thought . . .

He shuddered. Looking into the eyes of that tall, terrible man with the huge rifle was like looking into the eyes of Satan.

These men had no compassion. This man had no mercy. This man would murder him in cold blood.

Oh, how terribly appropriate that expression was. Drayne had never understood it before. *Cold blood.* It sounded impossible. Anger was a blood of heat. There was no anger in this Montana vigilante. Only a deep and bitter coldness.

Drayne looked into the face of death. He was frightened. But he was no longer the fearful, timid little rabbit he had been when he bolted away from the reaching hands in that Montana way station. Panic and timidity had been burned away in a forge he had been forced to enter by this very man and by all the others just like him. The ones who would shoot a man down when they might have reasoned with him instead. The ones who would chase a human being with dogs and bullets when they might have talked. Drayne felt a surge of heat into his face and a swelling in his neck and shoulders.

He was a man, and he would not stand and wait docilely to die.

He squared his shoulders and faced the would-be killer with dignity.

"I've done nothing to be ashamed of," he said. He said it for McKelty's benefit. There was no one else here that he cared about. Oddly, though, he cared very much what McKelty thought of him. "I'll not allow you to make me less than a man."

The lean, cold man was going to kill him anyway. Drayne could see that in the hunter's eyes and in the tic that was fluttering the flesh of his cheek.

So be it. If die he must, at least he could do so with his pride intact.

He nodded to the hunter slowly. Then grabbed for a rifle someone had left leaning against the front of the bar. Bryan Drayne had never in his life shot a firearm. He had seen them used only rarely.

Now he had no choice.

He must fight or he must die.

He snatched at the weapon with a speed and a sureness of motion that surprised even him.

He would *not* allow . . .

Chapter 40

Whelan's Marlin bellowed, the sound filling the small saloon and echoing back off the walls and ceiling.

The heavy, soft-point slug intended for use on deer or elk smashed into the killer's chest, driving him to his knees and spinning him half around so that his back was toward Tom.

Whelan yanked at the lever beneath the receiver, feeding a fresh, bright-gleaming brass cartridge into the chamber.

"Don't . . . !" Whelan pleaded.

He did not want to kill this man.

Even though the murderer had killed Harry and Lou, Whelan did not want to kill him in return.

But the man gave him no choice.

On his knees, breastbone shattered and blood pouring over his stomach, almost certainly dying already, even now the killer viciously tried to kill again.

Even now with his last breaths in his lead-torn lungs, the killer reached again for the carbine propped against the bar front.

If the killer so much as laid a hand on the weapon, he might be able to fire it into the crowd huddled against the walls of the place.

Whelan raised the Marlin to his shoulder, took swift aim, and sent a final slug into the back of the killer's head.

This time the bastard went down for good.

He would kill no more.

Tom shook his head. His ears rang from the repeated concussion of the two gunshots in close confinement, and his eyes stung from the powder smoke that lay heavy and sourly acid smelling inside the room.

The men who had been unknowingly celebrating with the killer began to shuffle forward silently, their festive mood blown away by the bullets and the blood. Someone looked at the damage Whelan's shot had done and began to gag. He hurried out of the saloon, and several others discovered quick reason to leave also.

Whelan was shaking.

"I didn't . . . you saw what happened. I didn't want to do that. I wanted to take him back. You saw what he done."

"It wasn't your fault," said the aging man who had been standing with the killer earlier. In the past few seconds the rancher had seemed to age even more. His face was seamed and haggard now, pale where before he had appeared robust and friendly. Now he just looked old. "You say he was a murderer? I never would've guessed it. He seemed so . . . ordinary, I guess you'd say. Just . . . ordinary."

Whelan ran a hand over his face again and rubbed at smarting, watery eyes. "Ordinary? Not that one. Meanest sonofabitch I ever seen, and I thought I'd seen some bad men."

"Hell, I reckon," someone else put in. "You had him cold, mister. Dead t' rights. But he went for that gun anyhow. Would've kilt you sure if you hadn't done for him first."

"Who was he?" someone asked.

"Said his name was Drayne," McKelty said. "Called himself Bryan Drayne. Said he was a businessman from New York City."

"Businessman, shit. I bet he never gave his real name neither. He was a real killer, that one. Tryin' to murder right t' the last."

"Jesus."

Whelan turned away, leaving the men of Beale's Gulch to marvel at the killer's meanness and to try and guess who the man who called himself Drayne might *really* have been.

In the days and months and years to come there would be a good many guesses. They would all wonder which of the legendary bad men had come to Beale's Gulch under a false name and died there still carrying it. Some would say the man called Drayne was really Butch Cassidy. Or Jack Ketchum. Or Frank James. Or . . . the list was nearly endless. Whelan knew.

And really it did not matter who the man had been in life. Of all the men in the saloon right now and all those who would soon hear and begin the guessing game, Tom Whelan suspected he was likely the only one who did not honestly care who this Drayne had been.

Tom had done his best. He only shot when he had to. Now, like those other times, he wanted to put today behind him and forget.

Forget *what* he could, *if* he could.

But he was surely going to miss old Lou. He'd been a good man, Lou. Whelan would miss him.

He sighed. He still had to get those supplies, and it would be a long hike back to the roan and the rest of his gear. And Harry's widow needed to know about this day, and the rest of the boys needed to be called in, those who were still out searching for the killer.

Tom took one more look at the lifeless thing that lay on the floor. Already someone was talking about bringing in a camera before the body was moved. Whelan wanted no part of that. He only wanted to go home and get to his work.

But he felt all right. He had to admit that. He had done what was right, and he had no regrets.

He let the Marlin down to arm's length and turned to walk out of the now noisy saloon.

He had done what was right, he kept telling himself. He had only done what was right.